Everyone loves R

"This is Van Dyken's best yet."

—*Publishers Weekly*, Starred Review, on
The Godparent Trap

"Rachel Van Dyken is on my auto-buy list."

—Jill Shalvis, *New York Times* bestselling author

"Rachel Van Dyken will tear your heart out, slice it in half with a machete, and hand it back. Then, you'll thank her."

—Kristen Proby, *New York Times* bestselling author

The
Godparent
Trap

Also by Rachel Van Dyken

The Eagle Elite series
Elite
Elect

The Bachelors of Arizona series
The Bachelor Auction
The Playboy Bachelor
The Bachelor Contract

The Bet series
The Bet
The Wager

The Godparent Trap

Rachel Van Dyken

FOREVER

BOSTON NEW YORK

Copyright © 2022 by Rachel Van Dyken

Cover design and illustration by Sarah Congdon.
Cover copyright © 2022 by Hachette Book Group, Inc.

Hachette Book Group supports the right to free expression and the value of copyright. The purpose of copyright is to encourage writers and artists to produce the creative works that enrich our culture.

The scanning, uploading, and distribution of this book without permission is a theft of the author's intellectual property. If you would like permission to use material from the book (other than for review purposes), please contact permissions@hbgusa.com. Thank you for your support of the author's rights.

Forever
Hachette Book Group
1290 Avenue of the Americas, New York, NY 10104
read-forever.com
twitter.com/readforeverpub

First Edition: July 2022

Forever is an imprint of Grand Central Publishing. The Forever name and logo are trademarks of Hachette Book Group, Inc.

The publisher is not responsible for websites (or their content) that are not owned by the publisher.

Library of Congress Cataloging-in-Publication Data

Names: Van Dyken, Rachel, author.
Title: The godparent trap / Rachel Van Dyken.
Description: First Edition. | Boston ; New York : Forever, 2022. | Summary: "Colby is living her best life: as a beloved food blogger, she gets to fulfill her childhood dreams of exploring the world. Being constantly on the move suits her just fine after a series of heartbreaks have taught her that settling down is not in her stars. But Colby's world comes to a halt when she's named the co-guardian of her best friend's two adorable children. Not only does she need to put down roots-fast-but to honor her friend's wishes, she'll be sharing custody with the one man she can't stand being on the same continent as, let alone living in the same house as. There's nothing accountant-extraordinaire Rip values more in the world than rules and precision-except when it comes to his baby sister. Being named custodian of his niece and nephew is enough to upend his carefully organized life, and he doesn't need the added complication of his sister's irresponsible, flighty...albeit kind and gorgeous best friend. Rip doesn't trust Colby to take their new responsibilities seriously-and Colby can't believe Rip thinks toddlers will follow his strict routine. With no choice but to work together, Colby and Rip soon find themselves exchanging ledgers and catchy photos for play time and diaper duty. They're even, dare they believe it, getting along...and fighting an unexpectedly fierce attraction. Colby's afraid they're only playing house, but can Rip convince her the family they're creating is for real?"— Provided by publisher.
Identifiers: LCCN 2022004294 | ISBN 9781538720530 (trade paperback) | ISBN 9781538720554 (ebook)
Subjects: LCGFT: Novels.
Classification: LCC PS3622.A5854845 G63 2022 | DDC 813/.6—dc23
LC record available at https://lccn.loc.gov/2022004294

ISBNs: 978-1-5387-2053-0 (trade paperback), 978-1-5387-2055-4 (ebook)

Printed in the United States of America

LSC-C

Printing 1, 2022

To my boys, Thor and Rorik.
Without you guys I would never
have been able to write about the
chaos that is parenthood, and
I wouldn't want it any other way.
Love you, boys. You're my soul
(guess Dad's pretty cool too, ha ha).

CONTENT GUIDANCE

This book does deal with some triggers, including death/grief (specifically, death of parents and death of a sibling), ICU hospitalization, and some bullying. I hope that as an author I brought these things to light in a way that helps readers. Thank you for reading. I really appreciate you all and hope you have a positive experience. As always I'm here for you!

Hugs,

RVD

Colby

Present Day

I heard the front door shut with a soft click—but it may as well have been a nuclear bomb going off, which would have made sense considering the state of everything around me. The house was a mess, and there was no way I was getting it cleaned up before he saw the damage. After several arguments over nap time, I'd finally gotten the kids to bed, though by the looks of the house, anyone would think a war had broken out before and after the event.

I sprinted into the kitchen, nearly taking out my right hip against the granite countertop, and furiously rubbed at my cheeks, trying in vain to remove the flour I knew was still caked to my face from our baking experiment earlier.

I could hear his footsteps approaching down the hall. Closer... closer...

PROLOGUE

Great. Rip was going to be all anal and accusatory, questioning whether I could really handle things, and I was going to have to explain myself. Again.

"No, no, no," I whispered to myself as I quickly shoved all the cookies that weren't burned farther onto the counter where he would see them first and then grabbed the trash can. In went the burned cookies, the leftover flour, several cups of purple glitter slime little man had decided he had to make, and an indistinguishable brown lump that I hoped to God wasn't from the cat.

Stu, the aging tuxedo cat with arthritis, meowed at me and gave me a look that said he was about two seconds away from puking up a hairball again, and don't even get me started on a cat that needed diapers half the time because life made him "anxious."

"Shoo!" I tried to shove the cat away from the table he'd just jumped on, only to groan when he knocked a bowl full of slime onto the hardwood floor.

Footsteps sounded.

Stu abandoned me, you know, just like Rip did every single day when he went to work and left me in chaos.

And the house still looked horrific.

Panic flared in my chest, and suddenly all I could do was stand there and watch in horror as Rip rounded the corner in his pristine black slacks and ironed navy shirt. Not a dark wavy piece of jet-black hair was out of place. His green eyes locked onto mine and twitched.

Both of them, not just one, both simultaneously. How was that even physically possible?

His height dominated the dirty kitchen, making me feel small—and stupid, always stupid. He didn't say a word to make me feel that way—he didn't need to. His frown said it all.

Failure.

I was a failure as a mom.

Rip narrowed his eyes at me, and then he slowly took in the rest of the dirty kitchen with a look of pure horror and disbelief. "Did we get robbed?" He stepped closer to the counter to inspect the damage, and I warily noticed that his pristine loafers were mere inches from the slime that had oozed out of the bowl and was slowly attempting to take over the kitchen floor.

I glared at him. "Yes, and all they wanted to do was bake cookies and make slime—weirdest robbers ever, but don't worry, I'm sure the cops can figure things out by the very chaotic crime scene they left behind." I finished with a muttered "Jackass" under my breath; OK, so maybe it was less of a mutter and more of a verbal attack, but still. Come on!

PROLOGUE

He let out an exhausted sigh as the muscles of his forearms flexed, drawing my attention to his rolled-up sleeves and slightly tired look. Maybe, just maybe, his day had been as hard as mine. "Look, I don't want to fight again."

I deflated a bit. This situation was new to us both, and it's not like anyone had given us a parenting manual. It would have been nice, though. Why couldn't we just get along? I hung my head and mentally waved the white flag. "Me neither, it's been a long day."

He sighed in exhaustion, or maybe it was envy. Then again, I could be going crazy. "At least you didn't have to work all day."

And I was murdering him in his sleep—or at least holding a pillow over his face in a threatening manner. It didn't matter that he had at least forty pounds of muscle on me. I was scrappy and pissed and so exhausted I could easily sleep for a year straight.

He took another step.

"No, wait—"

Of course he didn't listen, which meant the minute his foot hit the mystery substance, his leg went one way and he went another.

Arms flailing, he slipped in the slime, then fell with a thump onto his ass. His briefcase went careening out of his hand and opened in midflight. Papers exploded out of it, scattering like snow. And because I'm the unluckiest person in the world, that same briefcase hit the canister of flour on the counter, sending it over his head with a whoosh and a final crack of doom as it hit the floor.

I hurried over without thinking. "Are you OK? I was trying to warn you and—"

My left foot skidded through the slime and I went tumbling onto his lap, my legs in an awkward kneeling position, hands bracing his thighs like I was ready to pounce. Our heads nearly knocked as he wiped his face and glared.

"S-sorry."

"Slime?" He tilted his head like he was curious, which made me pause; he didn't have a curious bone in his body. I was also mildly impressed he even recognized the noxious stuff, though I wasn't going to give him the satisfaction of letting him know.

"I was a scientist in another life," I offered lamely, trying to control my breathing. Did he have to be so attractive? So annoying? So perfect? Everything about Rip made me both homicidal and pitiful. I didn't even understand my own feelings at this point; then again, I was basically living a life of no sleep and chaos, so maybe this was normal?

"Purple glitter, though? Really?" he asked.

At least he wasn't yelling. Not that he ever raised his voice. Sometimes I wished he would, sometimes I wished he'd just react, one time in his life. But most of all, I wished that he would let himself mourn.

He hadn't cried yet.

The only time he'd come near me—held me—was when I had.

He was still giving me a strange look that I couldn't decipher, and I was thankful for the distraction from my thoughts. The flour made him look ridiculous but somehow also more approachable.

"What?" I didn't move.

"Your eyes." He licked his lips, and flour dust fell between our bodies. "I forgot how pretty they are up close."

It was as close to a compliment as Rip had ever come to giving me.

I fought hard not to stare down at his plump lips, at the way his tongue had snuck out to wet them.

Something about the intense closeness broke me, made me want to get closer, made me need his comfort more than my next breath. I leaned in, expecting him to back away, or make an excuse or remind me of his vow to never touch me for as long as we both shall live. A vow he'd made after the one and only time we went on a disastrous date. Yeah, he was a real charmer back then, just like now.

And yet I couldn't help the attraction I'd felt for him all those years ago.

Weeks ago.

Days ago.

He frowned, cradling the sides of my face.

This time felt different.

Altered.

Last time he'd been horrified by his own attraction to me.

Last time he'd been cruel.

Last time I'd written off any sort of hope we could be together.

This time, our foreheads touched on a rough exhalation.

This time, Rip Edison leaned forward and pressed a painfully slow kiss to my lips.

My breath caught as he deepened the kiss, tasting me like I was a chocolate sample he wanted to devour, and then as soon as I wrapped my arms around his neck the sound of a cry filled the air.

We quickly broke apart.

"Not it!" we declared in unison.

I gave him a look.

He sighed and then gave his head a shake and gently lifted me off his lap, rose to his feet, and headed upstairs to the kids' rooms.

ONE

Colby

Nearly Three Weeks Ago

"Stop glaring at him like you want to set him on fire." My best friend, Monica, nudged me with her elbow, causing my glass of champagne to splash all over the front of my dress.

My life, ladies and gentlemen.

I mean, if I didn't have paint or a weird stain on my clothes, it was rare—as a fully functioning thirty-two-year-old you'd think I'd be all sleek lines, no student loan debt, designer purse, and a standing date to lunch with the girls.

Ha ha.

Not my life.

I glanced around at the few remaining guests at my best friend's house. At least I'd done something right. The night had been a success, even though I'd had to work with my least favorite person in the world to get it accomplished.

Rip had commented on more than one occasion as we plotted and planned this surprise party that I looked like a disaster waiting to happen. To my face, which really wasn't fair since I worked from home, so whom did I need to impress? And when I wasn't holed up on my couch, my laptop and a bag of takeout by my side, I was traveling to amazing resorts and sampling five-star restaurants for my travel blog. I had a life, and I lived it the way I wanted.

It wouldn't matter if I were a senior partner at a law firm or running for president, though, because to Rip I would always be a massive disappointment, or at least that's how he always made me feel, like someone who didn't have a real job or any sort of direction in life post-college.

And anyway, who was he to judge? I mean, could he really be that happy being an accountant? Ironing his jeans and crunching numbers? The thought alone made me break out in a cold sweat.

Luckily for me, his opinion had never mattered. I liked the freedom that came with my job—I could work from anywhere, anytime I wanted. It didn't tie me down to any place or any thing. And OK, sure, it didn't necessarily make it easy for me to settle down like Monica, or any of my other friends from college who just so happened to have mortgages, pets, and a lawn, but I was OK with that. Mostly.

I sighed.

Monica let out a giggle next to me. "Still such a klutz."

"Um…" I took a large gulp of what was left of my champagne and ignored the way Rip's green eyes seemed to assess every part of my suddenly too-naked-feeling skin. Ugh, I knew I should have gone for something more turtlenecky. Instead I was in a sleek black number that made me wish I had leg warmers and a cardigan covering every inch of my exposed body. "You hit me, your fault."

Her brown eyes lit up as she smirked at me. "Then maybe you should drink your champagne faster so you have enough liquid courage to walk up to Rip and tell him how you really feel without puking on his shoes."

I nodded solemnly. "Good plan. I'll just let him know I want to strangle him with my bare hands or take scissors to that perfect hair and clip the curl that refuses to straighten behind his ear."

"Must you fixate on the curl again?" she teased. Her perfectly tanned skin glowed in the moonlight as her curly brown hair bounced at her shoulders.

I deflated, and for a tiny second, I wanted to bolt in the opposite direction. Her brother was my opposite in every way that mattered.

3

I was pale skinned with hair that wasn't sure if it was blond or brown.

He had jet-black hair, light-green eyes, and, thanks to his naturally golden-tanned mama, the most gorgeous skin I'd ever seen up close in real life.

Monica draped an arm around me, and a fabulous new designer scent wafted between us. "Come on, he's not that bad. He's just... controlled."

I snorted into my champagne and let the last drop fall on my tongue. "He told me I was the worst date he'd ever had—and then he proceeded to tell me that he'd been on a blind date with a girl who would randomly shout, 'I want to have your babies' like her ovaries had taken over her voice box and common sense."

Monica's red lips pressed into a line before she burst out laughing. "Yeah, that one was my fault. Met her at yoga, liked her purse, bad judgment call. I thought she was just... peppy."

"Ya think?" I snorted and tried not to stare at his fit body in that black suit or the way he seemed to own the room without even trying.

People just naturally flocked to Rip.

Women found reasons to touch him.

And I wanted a reason to just dig my hands into his hair and mess it up.

"Building up courage?" Brooks, Monica's husband, wrapped an arm around each of us and stared ahead at Rip. "Tell me again about the time you spilled wine on his crotch. It's my favorite story."

I flicked his arm away in annoyance. "Remind me why I'm friends with you two again?"

"Because you love us!" Monica blew me a kiss and then detached herself from her husband. "Thanks for watching the kids again tonight. It's been so long..."

"So long," he echoed. "Because we both decided two-minute shower sex doesn't count—"

"No," she interrupted. "I decided that when you say hurry, get there, it takes away all of the romance, and when your kids are banging on the bathroom door, it's kinda hard to feel blissed out."

"Mommmmmyyyyy, I need my Lucky Charms!" Brooks said in a perfect imitation of their three-year-old, and then, "I'll be your lucky charm." All low and seductive.

"Yeah, could have gone my entire life without witnessing this moment." I pointed between the two of them. "Why are you even still here? It's your ten-year anniversary! Go eat Lucky Charms and have your weird shower sex!"

Monica's face fell. I knew what she was going to say before she even said it. "I feel guilty leaving the kids."

5

"They're both upstairs sleeping," I pointed out since I'd been the one to read *Brown Bear*, only to have Rip come into the room and tell me I was doing the voices all wrong. "Besides, Rip and I have this covered. Remember, we did manage to plan a surprise party and getaway for you guys without you knowing."

Barely, just barely, without killing each other.

"Oh, I knew." Brooks nodded, and his long, messy brown hair fell over his forehead, making him look more boyish. "I just knew you wanted it to be a surprise, so I let you have your fun. You can't keep secrets, Colby, ever since you cheated your way out of the math compass test at UW."

"You promised never to mention that again!" I glared accusingly.

He stirred the air between us with one hand. "This is why we're all best friends. We take secrets to the grave."

"Right, but you just outed hers, so..." Monica shook her head. "All right, we'll get moving. I'm going to give the kids another kiss, make sure Rip knows not to bother you too much—"

"I can handle Rip," I lied. But Rip and I had already made a pact months before when we started planning this anniversary surprise. We each did our jobs and that was it, no contact. It was easier that way after what had gone down between us last fall.

After I misread the situation, tried to kiss him, and was nearly clipped by a bike courier trying his damnedest to get his pizza delivered on time to the next-door neighbor.

It was a mistake.

Our date.

Our almost-kiss.

I sighed. "Like I said, I can handle Rip. You guys go kiss the kids good night again. You're only going to be gone a week, and you deserve this! Rip and I will clean up, make sure all the guests get home safely." Half the guests had already left, because hello, parenthood; when a party went past nine the parents started dropping like flies. "Just have fun."

"Thank you." Monica's eyes welled with tears. "You're the sister I never had."

"But," a smooth voice chimed in, "that's because God gave you the best brother in the universe."

I was shocked that I was able to keep a straight face as Rip bent down and kissed his sister on the forehead, then pulled his best friend in for a hug. I would never understand the bromance between Brooks and Rip.

"Thanks, man, we appreciate it." Brooks looked between the two of us, his expression weary. "No fighting in front of the kids."

"We don't fight," we both said defensively.

"Right." Brooks held up his hands. "Just...use your words, and if necessary the kids have puppets upstairs. I find sometimes it's easier to express yourself when—"

Rip flipped him off.

I nodded my agreement.

And then they were gone.

"So." Rip turned his megawatt grin toward me. "I'll take care of the kitchen, you got bathrooms?"

"If you hand me a plunger I'm going to shove it down your throat." I injected so much sweetness into my words he might have gotten a cavity.

He didn't even flinch. "You think it would fit?"

"I hate you."

"Same." His grin was calm, collected, beautiful. "I think one of the guests had an issue with the shrimp. Try not to make the mess worse."

"I think I can manage some indigestible shrimp."

"Oh, he digested it all right," was the last thing Rip said as he walked off and started saying goodbye to guests and talking with the caterer.

One week.

I could handle Rip for one week.

Besides, I had two adorable children to distract me.

TWO

Rip

I wasn't a kid person.

Not that it should come as a shock to anyone when they took a look at me, but something about my niece and nephew holding their stuffed animals close, their faces so peaceful as the glow from the unicorn night-light danced across the ceiling, hit me right in the gut.

I leaned against the doorway and smiled as Ben yawned and then flopped onto his stomach, his *Star Wars* pajama pants hiked up his skinny legs and his brown hair a tangled mess that I knew I'd have to fix before preschool in the morning.

Viera, his younger sister, refused to sleep in her room, which meant Ben had a tiny space on the far side of the double since she refused to sleep vertically.

I yawned behind my hand and closed the door, leaving it open an inch in case either of them needed us.

For a brief second, I thought about grabbing a pillow and blanket and just guarding the door like the paranoid uncle I was, but Monica had given me the don't-spoil-them look. She knew it was only a matter of time before I snuck into their room, built a tent, and let them sleep in it for the next week while their parents were in Mexico.

With a sigh, I started down the hall to my assigned guest room next door just in time to see a grumpy-looking Colby sway her way up the stairs.

"Tired?" I asked.

Everything about her bothered me, mainly because she was this force of nature that refused to follow any rules but her own.

Rules kept people safe.

"Yes," she hissed, her eyes narrowing into tiny slits until she looked behind me at the cracked door. Her face softened. "Let me guess, Viera's barely giving poor Ben any bed space."

I gave her a small smile like a temporary white flag—the only safe space for us was where the kids were concerned. "She's a bed hog just like her mom."

"Ugh!" Colby laughed. "Don't remind me, I had to room with her in college. The woman doesn't understand the meaning of shared space."

I chuckled.

And then we were back to the silence.

And the staring.

And the awkwardness where words should fill the air but all we could do was stand there staring at each other.

"I was just gonna...," I said finally, pointing to my room.

"Yeah, yeah," she said quickly. "Same. I just wanted to wash off the lovely shrimp bath I took—"

"Mommy!" Ben screamed. "Mommy! Mommy!"

I jogged back to their room, tripping over stuffed animals and Legos in an effort to get to Ben before he woke his sister, and Colby was right behind me.

"Buddy." I held out my arms.

He leaped into them, sobbing. "I miss Mommy!"

"Oh, Ben." Colby rubbed his back while he clung to me, his skinny arms tight around my neck. "They're going to go to the ocean, and tonight they're at a fancy hotel eating chocolate!"

"Chocolate?" His sniffles stopped. "Does that mean we get chocolate too? To be fair?"

I laughed as little Viera just slept right through it all. "What do you think, Colby? Do we get chocolate?"

Colby's grin was so wide, so spontaneous, that I

almost had to look away. When she smiled like that I forgot all the reasons she annoyed me. "Hmmm, how about if you sleep really good tonight, Uncle Rip and I will make you guys Nutella pancakes in the morning?"

"Really?" His eyes widened as he looked between us. "You mean it?"

"Yup!" I answered for both of us. "But you have to sleep super good and take care of your sister, all right?"

"I'm protecting her from the monsters," he announced as he puffed out his skinny chest. "They're scared of my roar."

"We're all scared of your roar." Colby nodded seriously. "It's so loud!"

He opened his mouth.

I covered it quickly. "Remember, Sister's sleeping."

"Oh, sorry, forgot." He gave me a sly grin. Lies, all the lies. Damn, I loved this kid.

"Bed," Colby said in a stern voice. "And dream of chocolate."

"Like chocolate fountains?" he asked. "And chocolate bathtubs?" He giggled at his own joke.

"Yes," I said as I tucked him back in and kissed him on the forehead.

Colby kissed both kids as well.

Ben yawned. "'K, happy chocolate dreams!"

"Happy chocolate dreams," Colby whispered.

"Happy chocolate dreams," I echoed.

And then we were back in the hall.

The mood shifted from loving and teasing to tense as hell.

"See ya in the morning." I gave her an awkward pat on the shoulder. "And try not to burn the pancakes."

"Says the man who burned the waffles last Sunday when the Hawks were playing?"

"The game was on," I pointed out, still annoyed that she'd spent nearly every Sunday with us since she and Monica bonded during childhood. Family day was just that. For family. And yet Colby was always there. Always.

"Uh-huh." She shrugged and winked. "See you in the morning."

"Yup." I turned around and absolutely did not look back over my shoulder to see if she was watching me, just like I didn't lie in bed for the next hour tossing and turning and wondering what had set us off on opposing sides in the first place. I mean, apart from the mess of her life, which drove me completely batshit crazy, it's not that she wasn't likable, or nice.

Part of me wondered if the issue was that I'd been responsible for Monica since our parents died. And up until she'd met Colby, the two of us had been enough. We were family. Our only family. And family meant everything to me. But then came Colby, and then Brooks and Monica got together and had a family of their own. Where did that leave me?

I wanted what Brooks and Monica had. I'd always wanted it. A normal life where I came home to my wife and kids. Stability. A dog. All the things Colby sneered at with her stupid jet-setting who-knows-where-life-will-take-me attitude.

I turned on my side and stared at the wall.

She was probably on her phone like always, wishing she were somewhere else, when there was nowhere else I would rather be.

THREE

Colby

Something wet hit my cheek.

I shoved it away, only to realize it wasn't a thing but a person, a tiny person with something wet in their hands. Perfect.

Please let it not be poo or pee.

I cracked open an eye to see Viera sitting next to me, her wet diaper in hand. "Look, I only went pee once!"

The potty training was not strong with this one.

"Yay!" I tried to sound excited. "Did you come in here to show me?" Had she touched my face with that thing? Horror washed over me.

"Yup!" She giggled. "Mommy says to. I get a prize when I don't go potty at night and use mine!"

"So no prize today." I was seeing double, what time was it?

I grabbed my phone.

Six a.m.

How was she so awake?

"No prize?" Her eyes filled with tears.

"Wait!" I grabbed the heavy diaper and dropped it onto the floor; it made a loud thunking sound against the hardwood. Yeah, I would need to clean that up later, but I was too tired to do more than think about it now. "If you cuddle for a few more minutes, then Aunt Colby will give you a prize at breakfast!"

"A *real* prize?"

"Awesome prize, huge prize, prize of your life." I was already pulling her next to me and tucking her into the bed. After a few seconds, I realized that the diaper was no longer on her, duh. "Wait here, I need to grab a pull-up, OK?"

"'K." Her eyes blinked heavily up at me. Yeah, she was dropping like a fly.

By the time I grabbed a pull-up from her bathroom and was back in my room, she was already sound asleep.

I carefully drew the covers back and got the pull-up over her tiny body, then crawled under the blankets and held her against my chest.

For a few brief moments, all I thought was, *This is perfect.*

"Slept in?" Rip said an hour later when I came downstairs with Viera in my arms. I'd at least gotten her dressed in a pink jumpsuit, while I still wore the black Nike joggers and ratty Yankees T-shirt that I'd worn to bed.

I didn't answer, just held out a coffee cup and grunted.

He shook his head and poured me a coffee, then took Viera from my arms, gave her a little twirl, and sat her in her chair.

My ovaries did a little jump at how good he was with children. I mean, he could be Satan to me any day, but the way he loved those kids, it almost made me forget how horrible he was.

Almost.

"Actually..." I took a sip of black coffee and felt the tension dissipate from my body. "Viera woke me up at six a.m. to show me her diaper."

Rip's eyebrows shot up. "And?"

"Oh, it was wet," I said into my cup. "My cheek can attest to that fact."

He snorted out a laugh and then gave Viera a high five. "It's all right, pretty girl, we'll work on it."

She gave him a toothy grin and kissed him on the cheek.

I watched the exchange with rapt fascination as he

17

tucked a curl behind her ear and then nuzzled her nose with his.

He hadn't shaved yet this morning, which made him seem ruffled and a bit out of sorts despite the fact that he was wearing a long-sleeved black Henley and skinny jeans tucked into black shiny boots that probably cost more than my car.

He was even put together on his off days.

I cringed when I looked down.

Oh well, take me as I am or don't take me at all.

Ben looked up from his iPad. His five-year-old face was covered in hazelnut spread. "You didn't do your hair."

"Thank you," I said through clenched teeth, "for pointing that out."

"She never does her hair," Viera announced proudly.

I squeezed my eyes shut. "Kids."

"She's not wrong...," Rip just had to mutter.

I shot him a glare while he started piling up pancakes on Viera's plate and cutting them into such perfect squares I wondered if he was measuring them with his knife each time he made a slice.

"Gonna cut up my pancakes too, Rip?"

"No," he said without looking up. "I figured you'd

just tear into them with your teeth, you know, like the animal you are."

"It's too early for you." I grabbed a pancake and shoved half of it into my mouth and was about to jab another with my fork when my cell started buzzing in my pants pocket.

I ignored it, and the call went to voice mail.

Then it buzzed again.

With a sigh, I swallowed my last bite and pulled out the phone. The number on the screen didn't look familiar, but something told me to answer it anyway. Heaven forbid we forget about the PTA meeting this week or the fact that I had to somehow make cupcakes for Ben's class in the near future.

Gluten-free. Nut-free. Dairy-free. *Can't wait. Can't freaking wait.*

And when I say "make," I mean "purchase from Whole Foods."

I tapped the phone. "Hello?"

"Is this Colby Summers?"

My stomach dropped to my knees at the solemn tone of the woman's voice, and I looked up at Rip. "This is she."

"Hi, Colby, my name's Kelly Smith. I'm the charge nurse at Mercy Grace. There's been an accident."

"Accident," I repeated, and then quickly ran into the living room as my world tilted sideways. "Is everyone OK? Who's this concerning?"

The line was quiet, and then, "We really need you to come down here and sign a few things."

Signing didn't sound bad.

"You mean fill out insurance forms?"

"I'm so sorry, Colby, I am, and I wish I was there to tell you in person, but you're the emergency contact for Monica Jones."

Rip walked into the room, his face lined with concern.

Somehow I managed to keep standing as I whispered, "Yes, I'm the emergency contact for Monica. Can you please tell me—" My voice cracked. "What is this about?"

"I'm so sorry to be the one to tell you this—there was an accident, the rain made it slippery this morning, an elderly gentleman sideswiped a car, forcing it into another lane. It collided with a semi."

Tears slid down my cheeks. "Was Monica in the car?"

"Yes, ma'am, Monica and her husband, we're trying to get in touch with his emergency contact right now."

Just then Rip's phone rang, and he pulled it out of his pocket and answered.

I knew what they would say.

I knew who was calling him.

I whispered in a gutted voice, "Were there any survivors?"

"I'm sorry, Colby, but no. We need you to come down and identify the bodies—"

The phone slipped from my hand, and then I saw nothing but darkness.

FOUR

Rip

Four Days Later

My life had spun completely out of control.

My best friend was dead.

My *sister* was dead.

I shuddered as I looked up into another pair of sad eyes. Monica's next-door neighbor. Sobbing.

I couldn't do this much longer.

"Mrs. Harris." I dipped my chin.

She reached down and hugged me, nearly tipping my whisky out of my hand as she patted me hard on the back. "I'm so sorry for your loss. I still remember when they moved in and I brought over cookies. She was just so sweet to invite me in and—"

"Thank you," I interrupted tersely, "for your kind words, but if you'll excuse me, I have to go check on the kids."

"Oh!" She clapped her hands against her cheeks dramatically. "Those poor kids." Leaning in, she lowered her voice. "Whatever will they do without their parents? And no grandparents to take care of them? You know, I was watching the news one time and this lovely boy lost his whole family in a fire and he went into the system! Can you imagine?"

I forced a polite smile. "Yes, well, that's not going to happen to Ben and Viera."

"Oh, well—"

"Rip?" Colby's eyes were bloodshot, her pale face stained with tears. "Ben won't come out of his room. He says he..." Her eyes flickered to Mrs. Harris and back. "He says he wants to see his daddy and, long story short, last year at Christmas his dad gave him a recording of his favorite book and he's wondering how he can hear his dad but not, but not"—she hiccupped—"see him in heaven."

"I'll take care of it," I said quickly, taking her hand and leading her away from Mrs. Harris.

Colby pulled her hand from mine and started to softly cry again as we made our way up the stairs.

"Stop," I hissed.

Her blurry eyes blinked up at me, mascara yet again making its way down her puffy cheeks. "What? Stop what?"

"*This,*" I leaned in and whispered. "You're making a scene."

She jerked to attention. "I'm. Making. A. Scene."

"Yes." I lifted my chin. "The last thing we need is the kids more upset."

Her nostrils flared. "Their parents just died, Rip! Crying is a natural reaction to devastation and heartbreak, not that I expect you to even understand the concept of emotion. How can you be so cold? Brooks was your best friend. Monica was your sister. They're *dead.*"

"I know who they were. And I know what happened to them. I was there at the hospital, remember? When we had to identify the two best people I've ever known, and you passed out and made it about you like you always fucking do!"

She gasped.

"Sorry." Shit. "Sorry, I just, I need you to be different."

"'D-different'?" Her pretty blue eyes searched mine. "What do you mean, 'different'?"

With a curse, I held out my hands at her black peasant dress and ridiculous blue feather earrings. "Honestly? Anything but this..." I waved my hand around in her general direction. "You're not traveling the globe writing about the best foodie destinations and drinking all the free wine you can get anymore. You're a parent now, so start acting like one. Otherwise I will file for full custody."

"You monster!" She gritted her teeth. "How dare you judge the way I grieve? The way I live—?"

"Why not? You do the exact same thing to me, and I'm the one handling this. I'm the one meeting with the lawyers, figuring out the house situation and everything else that you fail to understand matters."

"So cheering up the kids doesn't matter?"

"Not when you fill their heads with lies about magic and fairy tales and seeing their parents again, and how if they just talk out loud their mom and dad might hear them." I sneered. "It has to stop, Colby. Right now. Do you understand?"

She took a breath and jabbed her finger into my chest. "As long as you understand that I'm not going anywhere. And that if you want to survive under one roof with me and those two kids upstairs, you better stop acting like the jackass we all know you to be. Your sister would be ashamed!"

I eyed her up and down and snorted. "Between the two of us, who do you think she'd be ashamed of again?" I leaned in. "You have a wine stain on your dress and can't keep from making a scene in their house. Go sober up, I'll take care of Ben."

"I *am* sober!"

"You're sad. Even when you're trying to be an adult you're so off base, I just assume you're drunk." I moved past her toward the kids' rooms.

Past the pain slicing through my chest.

And the look of absolute horror and hurt on her face.

It made me feel better momentarily, to project all the confusion and anger I felt on the inside onto the only person available in that moment.

I was a fixer.

But I couldn't fix this. I couldn't fix any of it.

I couldn't bring them back to life. I couldn't make Colby into an actual adult. But I could talk to Ben. I could hug him. And rather than fill his head with fairy tales and lies, I could help mold him into the person Monica would want him to be.

Starting fucking now.

FIVE

Colby

I woke up to something fluffy rubbing my face, then startled awake when a rough tongue licked my cheek.

"I'm up, I'm up!" I lifted my arms over my head and stared directly into Stu's creepy cat eyes. "You."

Stu lifted his chin as if to say, *Yes, me, time to eat!*

With a groan I got to my feet and looked around the messy kitchen. I'd fallen asleep on the couch like an idiot. I'd planned on cleaning up from the wake last night, but I'd been so tired that I'd promised myself a quick power nap first.

The power nap had lasted a solid eight hours.

Suddenly my chest tightened as panic seized me—I knew what Rip would say if he came downstairs and saw the mess along with my state of disarray. Could I do nothing right? And why was it still so damn important that I impress him when I knew it was a futile task? His words from last night came back full force as my eyes truly focused on the living room, the kitchen, and the cat.

He'd been so hurtful. So mean. He'd always been annoyed by me, but he'd never been truly mean like that. Worse, it was like he'd reached into my soul and pulled out every single insecurity I've ever had and voiced it out loud.

I had no time to focus on his shitty behavior now, though, if I was going to get the mess cleaned up before he came downstairs.

I stumbled over my tossed heels and walked like a zombie toward the cupboard that held the cat food.

With a yawn, I grabbed a scoop and put it in Stu's bowl, then gave him a pat on the head before the pitter-patter of feet reminded me that I had bigger responsibilities than caring for a cat.

I'd known all along that Monica and Brooks had designated me Ben and Viera's guardian in their will. What I hadn't known? That they'd also chosen Rip as a guardian.

And that we legally couldn't split the kids up. Not that either of us would have wanted to; we weren't monsters.

Neither of us wanted to move the kids away from their comfort zone after the trauma of losing both parents, and since their house was paid for, it just made sense that Rip and I would move in.

I'd packed everything I owned into two suitcases, while Rip had pulled up with a moving van.

We'd argued over that stupid van before it had even arrived.

He'd wanted to move some of Monica and Brooks's things out to make room for his own stuff, and I'd told him something like *over my dead body*. The kids needed familiarity.

Rip, however, didn't like the clutter.

We finally compromised, with him agreeing to wait a few months before turning the house into his OCD heaven as long as I promised to attempt to be less like myself.

A hot mess who didn't know how to adult.

I winced as I looked around the kitchen where a lot of the food from the night before still lay on the counter, now completely inedible.

"I want eggs!" Ben announced as he ran down the stairs. "Can you make two?"

"S-sure." I licked my lips and turned just as Viera stumbled down the stairs with her blue stuffed dragon and blanket, her eyes full of sleep and her dark curly hair spilling over her shoulders onto her Elsa pajamas.

She looked how I felt.

Rough.

"Come here, Viera." I picked her up and put her on my hip, then opened the fridge door to grab an egg and groaned. Fantastic; the fridge was nearly empty.

I heaved Viera up on my hip again, grabbed the semiheavy carton of eggs, and shoved the fridge closed with my bare foot.

Viera went from having her arms wrapped around my neck to being a complete deadweight as her mouth dropped open in a giant yawn. She rubbed her eyes and rested her head on my shoulder like she was going down for a nap.

"Hold on, Ben." I winced under her weight.

"I'm so hungry!" He banged his head against the messy granite countertop and came back up with what looked like chocolate sauce in his hair.

Great.

"I know, buddy, I know." Where was Rip? "I'm just gonna put your sister on the couch to sleep—"

"I wouldn't," he warned just as I tried to lay her down, only to have her eyes burst open with tears.

"Hey, it's OK, it's—"

A wail from the pit of hell escaped from between her tiny lips as I tried to bounce her up and down and hush her.

Ben continued to bang his head into the chocolate sauce.

A trickle of sweat ran down my back as I took in the complete chaos.

Panic rose in my throat as I held Viera close and walked back into the kitchen. OK. Breakfast it was. Now all I needed was a pan to toss the eggs into, multiple shots of espresso, and prayer beads.

"Buddy, where did your—" *Don't say mama…don't say mama.* I closed my eyes against the tears that had immediately sprung to my eyes just thinking of Monica. "Where are the pans, do you know? Could you maybe—"

With a dramatic sigh Ben hopped off the barstool and slowly made his way over to where I was standing, then pulled open a drawer. "You use the flat one."

I gritted my teeth. "Thanks."

"Aunt Colby, do you even know how to make an egg?"

"Of course!" I lied. I rarely cooked. My DoorDash app was constantly running and open. I embraced food delivery apps the way most people embraced religion.

With fervor.

Dedication.

And loyalty.

While my job might have been to visit crazy

destinations and eat at five-star restaurants, it also meant I was rarely home to cook, and while I was a great judge of food and locations, a chef I was not.

Viera's wails turned into soft cries as she rubbed her eyes.

I bent down and grabbed the pan—the flat one that the five-year-old master chef had pointed out—and set it on the stove, then flicked on the gas.

Nothing happened.

Ben sighed again.

Viera turned to watch in interest.

Thank God she'd stopped crying.

"Why is nothing happening?" I mumbled under my breath.

Ben rolled his eyes.

"Hey, no attitude." I pointed the pan at him, then set it down on the counter and tried the knob again. The flame finally caught, scaring the crap out of me, causing me to jump and Viera to drop her dragon directly onto the burner.

It went up in flames immediately.

"Oh God!" I yelled. "Fire extinguisher! Where's the fire extinguisher!"

"Nine-one-one! Nine-one-one!" Ben shouted over and over again as he stopped, dropped, and rolled.

"You're not on fire!" I yelled. "Bugsy is!"

"Bugsy!" Viera screamed. "You kill Bugsy!"

With Viera still in my arms I searched the cupboards as both kids started screaming for me to save Bugsy.

I was about to call the fire department when I was shoved out of the way by a shirtless Rip. He held the extinguisher over the stove and sprayed white foam over the flaming dragon.

The fire was out instantly.

"You killed him!" Viera sniffled again. "He tail!"

"S-sometimes dragons lose their tails...," I said lamely. "I'm so sorry, Viera, it was an accident, why don't we go out today and get you a new Bugsy."

Her response was a shriek that nearly shattered my eardrums.

Rip moved past me again and washed Bugsy off in the sink.

"He'll have a few burned spots, sweetheart," he said softly. "But sometimes dragons get hurt. But they breathe fire, so he's not scared. He's OK." He held poor scorched Bugsy out to her. "See?"

A tear slid down her cheek and she screwed up her face again. I braced myself for another eardrum-shattering shriek, but what came out of her mouth was worse.

"I want Mama." She said it on a sob that was half hiccup, and I felt my heart drop to the floor.

"I know." Rip's Adam's apple bobbed as he swallowed, and for a moment I almost felt compassionate toward him. And then.

"Please tell me you know how to at least work a stove and this was an accident brought on by sleep-walking, stress, day drinking—" The look he gave me was one of pure annoyance at my inability to use a stove and multitask.

"I do!" I argued. "Ben's starving and he wanted a few eggs so I grabbed the pan—"

"I found it for her," Ben announced.

Little traitor.

I narrowed my eyes at him. "Anyway, I was doing things one handed because Viera was crying and I was just trying." I took a breath. "I *am* trying, Rip."

His green eyes flashed before he muttered, "Try harder."

I'd nearly forgotten about the casseroles people had dropped off the day before until he turned exactly where I didn't want him to. Exactly where I'd placed the carton of eggs next to the stove. "Are these for breakfast?"

"Um...see, I have a good reason for them all being

34

out." I was going to have to lie, then somehow manage to make a billion casseroles during Viera's nap. There was no way I was admitting I fell asleep and left them out all night.

Too late; he reached out and touched one, then another. "These are all warm. When did you take them out of the fridge?"

"Right." I licked my dry lips. Great. I was going to have to fess up. "Ben, why don't you go change into your school clothes real quick while I have a chat with Rip."

"But what about my eggs?" He groaned and dramatically threw himself over the barstool.

"Today we're doing cereal, OK? The stove needs to be cleaned, but I'll let you have Fruit Loops."

"Yay!" Waving his arms, he began jumping around the room, singing, "I'm having Fruit Loops. Fruit Loops. Just...follow your nose!"

I knew Fruit Loops were reserved for special occasions, but if this wasn't one, then I had no clue what was.

A birthday?

Christmas?

"Be right back!" Ben announced, racing up the stairs.

I held up my finger to Rip when he sighed in annoyance for what felt like the second time in five minutes, and I quickly walked over to the couch, made Viera comfy, and flipped on *Sesame Street*.

"Yay!" She clapped her hands. "My favorite!"

"Stay," I commanded.

Like she was a dog.

The cat jumped up to sit with her, and I turned to face Rip.

His arms were crossed, and I finally noticed he was wearing low-slung black Nike joggers that highlighted every muscle.

I gulped and met his gaze. I was in yesterday's dress, most likely with swollen eyes and makeup streaked across my face.

"So." I braced myself, wringing my hands together. "I was exhausted last night, we all were. I told myself I'd take a quick power nap and accidentally slept through the night."

His cold stare wasn't helping my rising anxiety. "Why didn't you set the alarm on your phone?"

It was my turn to cross my arms across my chest. "I was tired, Rip, I wasn't thinking clearly, so the casseroles—"

"Are all bad," he finished with a curse. "The food that everyone so lovingly made for us just sat on the countertop while you slept. Am I hearing that right?"

"Don't talk to me like I'm a child," I hissed. "Everyone makes mistakes! It was a long day for all of us."

"Then don't fucking act like a child!" he snapped right back. "You can't even manage to cook an egg, let alone a dinner, so what's your plan? McDonald's every day? Burger King at night?"

Tears stung the backs of my eyes. "That's not fair. I'm in over my head, but at least I'm trying! Besides, what's your contribution? Bossing me around and criticizing me any chance you can get? God forbid your dinner come from a fast-food restaurant lest a french fry accidentally touch your nugget!"

His voice lowered as he leaned closer. "First off, I don't eat fries."

I clenched my hands into fists. "Shocker, wouldn't want to ruin your perfect physique, now would we?"

"Checking out the goods again?" His nostrils flared.

"I would rather set myself on fire than touch you again!"

"Sure." He snorted. "Whatever. I'm going to be late for work. Clean up this mess and try to keep Viera alive until I get back."

"Cool, so I get to stay and clean up everything, grocery shop so we have food to feed everyone, and manage to get Viera down for a nap, while what? You schmooze clients and have an hour-long lunch filled with wine and laughter?"

He frowned. "You really don't know what I do for a living, do you?"

"You're a fancy accountant. With a fancy car. And a fancy suit. With fancy words and a fancy, perfect life. Did I come close?"

He sneered. "You have no idea what you're fucking talking about! I work my ass off. Unlike some people, I have a real job."

"You jackass!"

"Swear jar!" I heard Viera yell in her tiny voice from the couch.

She'd heard me say "jackass," but Rip saying "fuck" went unnoticed? Unbelievable!

As though he could read my mind, he grinned and took a step forward, his body towering over me as he bent down and whispered in my ear, "Fuck."

I sucked in a breath. "You, you, you—"

He just grinned and chanted it under his breath the entire way back up the stairs while a clueless Viera clapped her hands to whatever song was on the TV.

Like she only had hyperhearing when it came to my voice.

Son of a...

I eyed the stupid jar full of dollars and change on the table and stuck my tongue out at it.

Living with Rip.

With this chaos.

I wouldn't be surprised if I'd be able to fund both kids' college before the end of the month.

"Bastard," I muttered under my breath, only to have Viera call me over to the couch.

"Something funny?" I wrapped an arm around her.

"Wha's a bastard?"

"If I give you a dollar, will you promise never to tell Uncle Rip?"

"Two." She nodded. "Two dollar."

"Fine."

"Yay!"

I ruffled her curls, then got up to grab cereal for Ben, eyeing the clock on the oven and letting out a groan.

It was only eight in the morning. Just another twelve hours until bedtime. I could make it.

Just then, Viera appeared at my knee, her chubby little hand covered in chocolate. Wait. I hadn't left chocolate in the living room. What could she have gotten into so fast?

"Aunt Colby, I go poop!"

Awesome.

SIX

Rip

"Whoa, who spit in your Cheerios this morning?" Banks, good friend, coworker, and full-time pain in the ass, stopped at my desk and lifted his mug to his lips.

I sighed. "Do you really think that's work appropriate?"

He blinked down at the mug. In big, bold letters it read, "I love to wrap both my hands around it and swallow." He grinned. "I mean, it's true."

I groaned. "You and your mugs."

"It brings joy into an otherwise perilous day saving people from their taxes, what can I say?" He moved farther into my office. He was wearing some sort of black skinny-leg trouser, a loud red tie, and a white button-down shirt that had peppers on it.

"And the shirt? Is that just to give people seizures?"

"Oh, this? No, this I do to piss you off. You'd probably die before wearing a pepper."

"You hear yourself when you talk, right?" I reached for my own perfectly normal black mug and took a sip of lukewarm coffee, then winced.

"I've been told my voice is soothing." He winked and ran a hand through his ridiculously long mop of brown hair and sat down. "So, you gonna answer the question?"

"Don't you have somewhere to be? Anywhere to be?" I wasn't in the mood for his constant verbal sparring, not after the morning from hell.

"I'm fine." Everything was fine. It *would* be fine. I just needed to learn how to adjust faster and how not to murder my new roommate.

See? Easy.

"You're literally gripping your coffee cup like you might use it as a weapon, and if you clench your jaw any tighter you're gonna pop a molar," Banks pointed out. "Seriously, take a break from the joy of numbers and talk to your best friend."

"We aren't best friends."

"Correction. Your best friend died. But I was next in line. So now I'm the new best friend, and before you get all pissed off again, that's exactly the sort of thing that Brooks, our mutual friend, by the way, would have said—at my fucking funeral."

I cracked a smile.

"Ah, there it is." He leaned forward, his white teeth blinding me with a knowing smile. "Now seriously, how can you be in such a bad mood so early in the day? Problems in suburbia?"

I groaned. "She's impossible!"

"Most women are."

"Heard that." Our coworker Olivia flipped him the bird as she walked past.

One day they'd finally hook up and relieve every single person in the office of the blatant sexual tension they refused to acknowledge.

That day was not today.

"Anyway..." Banks cleared his throat very loudly and rolled his eyes. "Let's discuss."

"Let's not."

"I think talking would help."

"If I wanted a therapist, I'd hire one."

"Best friends can be therapists." He grinned. "Let's start with the stick shoved so far up your ass that I'm worried you lack the ability to even order anything other than black coffee while you adjust your twice-ironed pants and judge the girl ordering the mocha."

"I don't—"

"You do." He sighed. "And honestly, since moving

into a five-bedroom house with a white picket fence two weeks ago, you've gotten worse."

"Have not!"

"Have." He jabbed a finger at me. "Look, man, I know you're mourning. We all are, but this wasn't just losing a best friend and a sister—this was losing them and not even getting time to grieve because of the kids..."

"Yeah." I didn't meet his eyes. "It doesn't help that Colby is a fucking mess!"

"The complete opposite of you, I'm aware, and so was your sister, who loved you and trusted you with her kids. So ask yourself, why would she punish you by making you coguardian? There has to be a reason she chose Colby."

"Punishment?"

"Try again."

I sighed.

"Can you really not think of one redeeming quality Colby has?"

"I woke up with Ben screaming 911, rolling on the floor, a little girl funding her college via a swear jar, and the need to use a fire extinguisher, so forgive me if I'm having a bit of an issue finding one thing she does right."

He was quiet, and then, "Do the kids like her?"

"Shit, they love her, it's like they have another kid around to play with!"

He winced. "I was thinking something more along the lines of 'She's really kind,' but OK, I guess that works too."

I ran both hands through my hair and tried to push this morning's disaster to the back of my mind.

Nope. Wasn't working.

The kids screaming. The *fire*.

How had Colby survived this long without a keeper?

"I think you're being a little too hard on her." Banks shrugged. "Especially if she's home taking care of Viera while you're here at work. That little girl has more energy than the Tasmanian Devil. Add that to doing pickup for the kids, taking care of the house—"

"Her version of taking care of the house is making sure the dishwasher is loaded, and then the clean dishes sit inside the dishwasher while the dirty dishes get piled in the sink until finally I can't take the mess anymore and I do it myself," I pointed out. "That's her version of taking care of things."

"So she's like a bachelor."

I snorted out a laugh. "She's worse!"

"All I'm saying is trust your sister's judgment and try, just try, to give Colby a chance. Do it for Monica. And for Brooks."

And just like that, my anger was gone. I ducked my head and started shoving papers around on my desk so he wouldn't see the trembling in my hands or the tears that had gathered in my eyes.

My sister. My best friend. They were gone.

Oblivious to my emotional shift, Banks shot to his feet. "Good talk," he said. "I'm here, you know...when you need me."

"Thanks, man." A bit of the tension in my neck dissipated as he waved me off and walked out of my office.

I stared down at my phone, immediately feeling guilty for the things I'd said to Colby, the hurt in her eyes haunting me...just a little.

"I'm trying!" she'd said.

But I couldn't possibly believe that she was trying her best.

Still, there was a reason my sister had adored her.

And a reason that Brooks, all that time ago, had told me I needed to get over myself and fucking make a move on the one girl who drove me to drink.

"Do it." Brooks and I had stopped off to meet the girls for happy hour. Colby had just gotten back from some resort in Mexico. Her skin was golden, her smile wide like she was well rested and excited about life, and I felt this ridiculous jealousy.

Why couldn't I be like that?

Relaxed?

Not so controlled?

Free. Why couldn't I be free?

Maybe I was drunk off her smile, but my brain told me if I just kissed her once, I'd feel that freedom, I'd be able to steal a bit of it for myself. I wouldn't feel so stressed out all the time. I'd dumbly admitted this to Brooks after one beer, and now he was shoving me toward her.

"No," I barked out. "Not happening. We'd be a disaster, hell, we are a disaster, every single interaction either ends up in a black eye, spilled drinks, hospital visits—"

"—Stop exaggerating."

"I'm not," I deadpanned, then stole a look at her again. She was adjusting one of her red heels, looking back over her shoulder.

Her blue eyes locked with mine and I forgot to breathe as tension swirled between us. She was wild. I was calm. She was my complete opposite. So why did I always feel like I was out of breath whenever she gave me that look? I told myself it was irritation.

But Brooks knew me like a brother.

It was infatuation.

With my sister's best friend.

My breathing slowed when I thought back on that day last year. I'd had no idea that less than seven months later, he'd be gone. And I'd be left with the one woman I didn't know how to deal with.

I let out a snort. I'd probably spend the rest of my life in the center of her chaos and never wear clean pants again.

Ever.

I shuddered.

No, thank you.

I picked up my cell and quickly shot off a text to Colby, waving the white flag as much as my ego would allow me.

> **Me:**
> Sorry for this morning.
> I know you're trying…

She responded right away.

> **Colby:**
> What's with the…? That's basically like saying, I know you're trying but…

I rolled my eyes.

> **Me:**
> Can't you just accept my apology?

> **Colby:**
> Was that one?

> **Me:**
> I'm sorry. There, is that better?

Colby:

Yes, I was especially touched when you asked if it was better. Thank you, I could feel you meant those words. Consider yourself forgiven.

I nearly threw my phone in frustration.

Me:

Sarcasm? How rare coming from you. Even in text form you just can't seem to help yourself, can you?

Colby:

Not when it comes to you, no. Wanna know what your name is on my phone?

Me:

I'm dying with curiosity.

Colby:

Ah sarcasm, coming from Ripped Pants, that's your name in my phone. Every night I go to sleep and imagine taking scissors to your closet. It's soothing.

Me:

Sorry, all I caught was that every night when you go to sleep you imagine me…

Colby:

Stabbing you, or wait,
your clothes, sorry, finger
slipped…

Me:

And we're back to the…

Colby:

I think my point was made.

Me:

If you say so…

Colby:

AHHHHHH

Me:

What's for dinner?

Colby:

I'd hide the knives, fair warning.

Me:

Then how will you use them to cook
for me? Something hearty sounds nice
btw, can't wait to see what you come
up with.

Colby:

I forget, is arsenic traceable by forensics if it's in smaller doses or should I just go for the hemlock?

Me:

I'm stunned.

Colby:

That I'm killing you?

Me:

No, that you actually paid attention in science.

Colby:

Both it is! See you tonight, honey!

Me:

My balls literally sucked back into my body when I read that.

Colby:

Funny, I didn't know you still had them.

Me:

They're huge.

I face-planted into my palm with a soft groan. *That's* what I'd gone with? "They're huge"? I watched in horror as she typed back.

Colby:

You know what they say about people when they're trying to convince others of things…

Me:

I guess you'll never know.

Colby:

Question, do you have sex with the lights off and your socks on every time or…

Me:

You're baiting me.

Colby:

It's killing you, admit it.

"Bro!"

A knock sounded at my door, and I almost jumped out of my skin. I quickly dropped my phone like I had been caught watching porn.

Banks hovered in the opening, grinning from ear to ear. "Who are you texting? Hot date? New woman? What's she look like, let me see—"

"No!" I scrambled to my feet and fumbled with my phone before sliding it into my pocket. "Did you need something else?"

"Burgers." He nodded. "I'm taking you to get burgers. And a beer. You need to let off some steam." He walked around my desk and put his hands on my shoulders, shoving me out the door. "But I warn you, if you use your fork and knife to eat the burger, I'm stabbing you, mmmkay?"

"That was one time."

"It was enough, buddy." He patted me on the shoulder, and I followed him out the door, my phone vibrating with another text.

I wasn't going to check. In fact, it brought me great joy that she'd be constantly checking to see if I'd responded.

"Whoever she is, I want to meet her one day...," Banks said once we were in the elevator going down.

"Huh? Who?"

"The girl on the phone, the one who as of two seconds ago still had you grinning from ear to ear."

I scoffed and literally had trouble hiding my smile, what the hell was wrong with me? "It was nobody."

"Sure. OK. Nobody." He hit me in the shoulder with his fist. "Nobody at all."

SEVEN

Colby

If I overthought things the way I usually did, I might assume that Rip had been flirting with me and freaked himself out and that's why he'd dropped the conversation.

But I knew better.

He'd truly meant what he said in that text. He wasn't a flirt, he was all business, straight to the point, even though I was momentarily stunned at his ability to fire back responses so fast. Did the man even work?

I smiled to myself. At least he had given me an apology, or a Rip apology. In all honesty the texts had made my day until—

Well, until he felt the need to explain how big his balls were. I'd half expected him to follow up with some mathematical equation explaining just how huge.

God, I bet he even got hot when a woman used terms like *tax compliance*.

I shuddered.

"Aunt Colby?" Viera tugged on the hem of my hoodie. "I hungry."

Shit.

I'd planned on going to the store but had been side-tracked by a toxic diaper, and other than cereal and fruit snacks there wasn't really much in the house to eat.

As much as I didn't want Rip judging me with that pompous sneer he had down perfectly, I pulled out my phone and DoorDashed some McDonald's.

"Chicken nuggets OK?" At least I was good at one thing, right? Using food apps. I wondered if that would hold up in a Rip argument. I mean, could he order from four different apps at the same time while monitoring the driver's progress and texting them specific instructions on where to leave said food?

I think not!

I set my cell faceup on the counter, then picked up Viera and sat her next to it. Her little legs dangled off the hard, sticky granite. "Your nuggets are getting made right now!"

She scrunched up her nose. "How they make nuggets, Aunt Colby?"

I gave her a serious look. "A nugget maker, of course."

"Ohhhhhhh." She nodded vigorously, her pretty brown hair grazing her shoulders. "What it look like?"

"Ummmm, like a chicken...stamp." I winced. "But bigger! So they can make more than one at a time."

There, that sounded like something McDonald's would do, right?

Her eyes went wide as saucers. "They stamp the chickens?"

"Oh, sweetie! Don't worry, the chickens are already dead."

Her lower lip quivered.

"No, no, no, no." I knew that look; it was the look of a three-year-old about to let loose. "Viera, I'm just kidding, the chickens are alive! They're all alive on a farm, living happy and chirping and—"

"CHICKEN NUGGETS ARE ALIVE?" she shrieked.

Oh dear God.

The front door slammed just as Ben walked in and covered his ears. My only saving grace was that today was jujitsu, and it had been Jake's mom's turn to take them after school, then return Ben back home.

"Viera!" he yelled, throwing his gear across the hardwood floor. "Stop screaming!"

Now both kids were yelling.

And I was sweating—again.

The DoorDash guy was probably going to call the cops and report me to child services.

"Chicken nuggets are *alive!*" she squealed. "With a chicken press!" The drama that followed as she threw her little body against mine was Academy Award–worthy.

I caught her so she wouldn't fall off the counter and held her tight, stupidly assuming that holding her would make her stop screaming when it only made it worse.

"HA HA!" Ben pointed. "You're growing chickens in your tummy, you're growing chickens in your tummy!"

"AM NOT!" she yelled, and then she stopped crying enough to look up at me with bright-blue eyes. "Am I growing chickens?"

Another quiver of her lower lip.

And then a knock on the door.

There is a God.

"Look! It's food, and you can have fries. I'll eat the nuggets, or your brother, who was just teasing." I shot him my best grown-up-in-charge glare and must have had it down well because his shoulders slumped as he kicked the chair in front of him and crossed his arms. "Right, Ben?"

"Maybe." Then he smirked up at us and put a hand on the top of his head and started doing the rooster dance. "Ca-ca, ca-ca, ca-ca—" His little feet skipped against the still-dirty floor.

Viera burst into tears again.

Just then the front door flew open. Rip held the McDonald's paper bag away from his body as if so repelled by the fast food that he didn't want it near his person or—God forbid—touching his skin. "Who the hell ordered McDonald's?"

Both kids pointed at me.

Ben spoke first. "Viera's growing a chicken."

Viera's voice was hoarse from screaming. "Chicken nuggets are alive!"

Rip gave me a what-the-hell look.

How to even begin to explain the escalation from DoorDash to this moment? I mean really?

I'd forgotten that I still had all our arts-and-crafts stuff out, which meant there were finger paint and wet pictures all over the table.

Dishes were piled high in the sink.

I followed his narrowed eyes to the milk that had

spilled out of this morning's cereal bowls and that still sat in a tidy little puddle on the kitchen floor.

"Did you even...shower?" Rip asked in a tone that made it sound a lot like *Is that dog shit on your shoe?*

I hissed out a breath. I didn't need his judgment. I knew what I looked like.

I was wearing the pair of sweats I'd grabbed from the floor while Viera was having her first of many freak-outs that morning. Did he even comprehend the herculean effort it took to make sure she was happy while putting on pants? Did he?

It was why moms wore leggings!

Nobody had time for real pants.

My white tank top had finger paint smeared on it, and my hair, which had seen better days, was currently in a messy bun on my head.

I could only assume it too had flecks of pink paint in it and possibly Fruit Loops.

Yay.

"No," I snapped. "Because keeping Viera alive seemed like the better grown-up decision!"

He gritted his teeth and tossed the bag onto a barstool by the counter in disgust, causing it to slide off said chair and onto the floor.

"That's the only food we have, you know!" I glared.

"That's not food!" He pointed at the bag in horror. "That's processed soy and God knows what else that takes over sixty days to digest fully in your stomach slammed together into the shape of a hamburger!"

Ben, being wicked quick, already had a fry in his mouth, then very quickly dropped it and made a face. "Why would you feed us that?"

"I'm huwngrrryyyyyyy," Viera wailed again. "But I don't want dead chickens!"

Ignoring the chaos, Ben swiped the bag from the floor and peered in. "What other food did you get?"

Nothing. Because he hadn't been here when I ordered.

Which meant I hadn't done a head count.

Which also meant Viera had dinner, but nobody else did.

According to Rip's annoying chore chart taped to the fridge, dinner was promptly at six thirty.

All eyes fell to me.

I grabbed my phone. "I didn't have time to get groceries, but, um, how do tacos sound?"

Rip rubbed his gorgeous eyes and leaned against the counter like he was seconds away from another lecture while Ben started stealing fries and nuggets with a shrug. "I like tacos." He added more fries to a mouth already full of food and munched.

"Aunt Colby!" Viera sniffled, her lower lip quivering again. "He's eating my french fries!"

"Am not!" Ben said defensively as a fry fell from his open trap and onto the floor.

"You're a liar!" She pointed. "Right, Uncle Rip? He gets in trouble for lying! That's two time-outs in the blue chair!"

"Suddenly glad we kept the chair and didn't move any furniture out of the house," I said under my breath, earning an exasperated look from Rip, who took Ben by the hand and led him into the living room, calling over his shoulder, "Order whatever, just make sure it isn't fast food."

He paused and then called back at me, "And remember..." His eyes softened in that moment and I almost imagined we were in this together. Instead he lifted his right eyebrow and continued, "I'm gluten-free."

He turned away then, so he didn't see my eye roll or the exasperation pulsing off me.

I always fell short.

And he always ended up on top.

And not in the good on-top way where toes are curling and your world is changing.

The kind where he was always looking down.

And I was never enough.

I was feeling sorry for myself and I knew it, but damn, after today's texting I'd expected at least a little bit more grace instead of judgment.

I swiped at the gathering moisture beneath my eyes, ready to defend myself or at least say something adultlike, when the doorbell rang again.

"It's the chickens!" Viera gasped.

"No, it's not, sweetie." I gave her a small smile and pulled her into my arms, carrying her to the door. Maybe I'd look as in over my head as I felt and the person on the other side would offer to babysit while I cried in the shower.

One could only hope!

After taking a deep breath, I opened the door and slammed it back again before the she-devil standing outside could utter a word.

"Who is it?" Rip called.

Viera started giggling. "You shut door hard!"

I felt my entire face pale as I reached for the door again with a shaking hand, only to have Rip move past me, taking Viera out of my arms along the way, and open the door himself.

"Hey there, hot stuff. You forgot this at the office. Figured you were just anal enough to get grumpy when you didn't have all your separate lunch containers."

The woman on the doorstep was wearing a full, expertly applied face of makeup that would make any glam squad proud. Her white pantsuit was molded to her body like it was made for her, and I'd bet my life that it was designer. She wore Chanel diamond earrings and a matching necklace and was tall enough to be an Amazon princess. She. Was. Stunning. Stunning and familiar.

"Oh! You must be Colby. It's great to meet you!" Her megawatt smile was everything that used to terrify me in high school. She handed Rip some plastic contraption that I'm assuming separated all food, then held out her hand to me.

I didn't even check to see if I had poop on my hand before I took hers.

Or any other horrible substance.

Because Heather Donnelly was standing at my front door—and she didn't even seem to recognize me. Then again, I wouldn't recognize me with a magnifying glass at this point in my life, but still.

I shook her hand—hard—and noticed how her smile wavered as she pulled back and wiped her palm on her sleek white pantsuit before forcing another smile and tossing her jet-black hair over her shoulder.

"Y-yeah, that's me." I tried for a smile, prayed to

God I had nothing in my teeth, and wanted to immediately hide behind Rip, not that he was any safer.

"I've heard a lot about you." She winked, her green eyes sparkling in a way my blue ones never would.

And of course she had the perfect wing-tipped liner and just enough red on her lips to look natural.

"All great things, I'm sure." I laughed awkwardly while Rip made a choking sound next to me.

"Yeah." She briefly looked away. "Entertaining at least, right, Rip?"

I shot him a look. At least he had the decency to look embarrassed.

"Yeah, well...," he started, and I could feel the tension rolling through his body as they shared a look that awkwardly made me feel like the third wheel. "Thanks for stopping by, Heather, but we were just having dinner, so..."

"Oh, no problem!" She winked. "See ya tomorrow, boss!"

With a wave she turned on her tall heels, which clicked against the concrete as she sauntered across the driveway and got into a Tesla as red as the soles of her Louboutin shoes.

"Can barely hear that thing even turn on," I whispered to myself in awe, and then I glanced toward the minivan in our driveway and felt my soul do a little whimper of jealousy.

"So." I turned toward Rip. "Heather Donnelly is your..."

"Receptionist and sometimes assistant." He actually looked uncomfortable.

Good. He should.

It wasn't like he didn't know.

"And you were going to tell me that the woman who made all my high school days a living hell was on your payroll when, exactly?" I seethed.

"It's my company, not yours, and she came highly recommended from—"

"Let me guess, Lingus Industries? The multimillion-dollar company her parents own? She doesn't even need to work!"

"She's changed." He cleared his throat. "And she likes to work. It gives her purpose. Something you would clearly know nothing—"

I narrowed my eyes and subjected him to a glare. "Finish that sentence. I dare you. I've been home while you've been at work getting a break from the chaos that is suddenly being responsible for two kids while mourning the loss of—" I stopped talking because Viera had suddenly gone really quiet. I'd forgotten she was even between us.

Her lower lip quivered. "Am I in trouble?"

"No, sweetie, I'm just...I'm really tired," I admitted. "Why don't you go tell Ben he can come out of time-out and you two can color a bit?"

Rip set her down.

She ran off, and I immediately grabbed ahold of his crisp white shirt with my dirty rotten hands and tugged him outside, leaving the screen door open so I could at least see the kids. "You get a break the minute you walk out this door in the morning. I haven't even started my own work today, and I have to post my articles at least three times a week. It's how I make money, it's what I enjoy, and I know I need to be here for the kids, but we need to figure something out, because I'm losing it playing fake mom all day, and you don't seem to care!"

"First off..." He leaned in and flicked a fleck of pink paint off my shoulder. "Before you get that murderous look in your eyes—yup, that one right there—remember why my sister entrusted her kids to you. Why people love you so much in general. You're the fun one, Colby. Second, don't you think I'd trade places with you in a heartbeat?" His eyes went completely glassy, like he was holding back tears. "They're gone. Gone." His voice cracked. "And those kids are all I have left in this world." His chest heaved, and I wanted so badly to say, *I'm right here. You have me.*

But instead I chose silence.

Which meant that as his eyes searched mine for any hint of compassion, all I did was stare back. Because wasn't that what you did when you were hurt? When you were so exhausted you couldn't see straight? When your grief felt so overwhelming you had no choice but to ignore it because two small children's tears were more important than yours and you couldn't justify your sadness in the face of theirs?

Even when you knew you needed those quiet moments too?

The ones where you screamed silently into your pillow, shattered whatever object you could find handy, and slid down to the floor in a heap of devastation?

"Neither situation is easy," I finally said, licking my lips, watching as his eyes darkened, as he took a physical step back, putting distance between us.

Rip ran a hand over his head, his jaw flexed tight like he was clenching his teeth as he looked down at the ground. "How much time do you need?"

"Time?" I blinked. "For?"

"Your posts or articles or whatever the hell you do. How much time do you need?"

"This feels like a trap."

"It's not a trap."

"It's you."

He smirked despite the heaviness between us, around us, lying at the ready to swallow us whole. "I can take a few days off, work from the house, you can use my office, get away, and then maybe you'll have some compassion for what it's like leaving your heart at the door every morning and wondering if you'll ever make it back to see their faces—and doing every damn thing you can to make sure you do—because you're it— *we're* it, Colby. We're *it*."

A tear slid down my cheek. He probably thought I was the weakest human on the planet, but he'd spoken my fear aloud, and it was terrifying. "You think about it too, then? What will they do if something happens to us? What if something happens to *them*?"

"Every day." He swore under his breath. "Every morning, every time I get in my car, every few minutes when I wonder if you're able to keep them alive..."

"Very funny." I gave him a slight shove. "I still hate you."

"Oh, this conversation changes nothing. It just means we're both helpless and sad—and you're still a hot mess."

"That"—I looked down at myself—"I can actually agree with right now."

He cracked a smile. "You'll see how hard it is to go to an office and, what did you say I did?" He made air quotes. "Get a break?"

I nearly growled. "And you'll see how hard it is to keep the cat from eating the goldfish—or to keep Viera from watching *Caillou* reruns until you want to actually find this magical cartoon person and kill them dead."

"All right." He held out his massive hand, and I blinked to get rid of the image of that hand pulling me close, comforting me. "It's a deal."

I grabbed his hand and squeezed—hard. "We need to figure out this godparenting thing. We need a plan. Something solid. Something that keeps the kids alive. That keeps *us* alive."

"A godparent plan? One that benefits us and the kids?" He was still holding my hand, and I was having trouble remembering why I wanted to punch him.

"Sure." I tugged my lower lip with my teeth. "The kids are pretty OK at the moment, considering. But we are not. We need to start working with each other, not against."

He nodded slowly, as if he was humoring me, and I tried not to let it piss me off. Instead I kept going.

"Starting tonight. The last man standing after all the chaos gets future time off, whether it's to go on a date, do a staycation here at the house barricaded in their room, or whether they want to order all the McDonald's their stomachs can take and fall asleep in the fries."

He made a face. "I don't want to even think about how many times you've probably done that in your life."

"Not telling." I dropped his hand. "Is it a deal?"

"Of course." He seemed to hover over me, or maybe he was just towering and I was mistaking it as a sexual hover like when you wanted to be close to someone but you didn't want them to know that's what you wanted. Ugh. What was I even thinking?

Focus!

"Great." I stumbled back a bit.

He nodded and then went back into the house, seemingly unfazed by the howling I could hear escalating in the living room.

The guy was perfect.

He'd probably have laminated schedules for everyone before the end of the week, proving again just how out of my element I was.

Before the neighbors could wonder why I was pacing and muttering to myself on the front porch, I was saved by the DoorDash delivery lady, who handed me something that didn't have gluten and something for the kids loaded with avocado and veggies that wouldn't earn me another judgmental stare and a snarky lecture about the food pyramid.

Once I'd served the kids their vaguely nutritious dinner, I started picking up the kitchen and nearly choked when Rip made his way over to the sink. We didn't speak, just stared into the dark window as we rinsed dishes and loaded the dishwasher.

We worked silently side by side, and as hard as I tried to avoid looking his way, his eyes finally caught mine in the reflection in the window. He didn't look pissed off for once. He looked down as soon as he realized I saw him looking at me, but I couldn't tell what he was thinking, and I desperately wanted to. Could he see how scared of all of this I really was? Or was he gearing up to mock my housekeeping skills again? I waited for the insult to come, the one that would break whatever tension was happening between us; instead he did something I hadn't seen him do since...well, forever. Rip Edison smiled.

EIGHT

Rip

I called Banks first thing in the morning, to let him know I wouldn't be coming in and that I was loaning Colby my office. She seemed genuinely excited to borrow it, but as I well knew, Colby's excitement could sometimes backfire. I didn't want Banks to get blindsided by her chaos, as humorous as that would be—for me at least.

He didn't deserve that level of terror.

He answered on the first ring and yawned loudly into the phone. "Yellow?"

I rolled my eyes. "Dad jokes only work when you're a dad..."

He barked out a laugh. "Had a woman call me daddy last night—that counts, right?"

"You're disgusting."

"Thank you, I can tell that really came from the

heart. Did you call me to shower me with compliments, or do you finally need your best friend for once? I'm great with kids. Could probably give Colby some etiquette lessons—in fact—"

"—Are you going to let me talk?" I cringed when I heard the pitter-patter of feet dashing across the downstairs floor followed by the sound of something breaking and then Colby yelling, "blue chair" and "time-out." "Colby's going to head over in a while to use my office."

I hoped, fast as I said it, that he'd only catch half of what I said because, let's be honest, he had the attention span of a fly. Instead he was quiet on the other end of the phone.

A rarity.

Miracle, really.

"Are you sick?" he finally asked, his voice incredulous.

"What?" I pulled back and stared at my phone, then put it back to my ear. "No, I'm not sick."

"Ohhhh, then you're working from home today?"

"No, well, I mean, I'll attempt to, but no. I came home last night to a disaster of one kid thinking she had live chickens in her stomach—long story—the other taunting her that she was going to die—even longer story—and the entire house in ruin. Colby was on the verge of tears and needs to hit her blog deadlines, whatever that means, so I offered her my office and we agreed to swap places for a week."

Banks burst out laughing and then sobered. "Oh shit. You're serious?"

"Of course I'm serious! Once she sees how—"

"Don't finish that sentence, bro. Actually, you know what? Let me just put you on speakerphone so every single parent within a ten-mile radius can hear you make an ass of yourself."

"Hilarious."

"I thought so. Anyway, seems like you need me."

"What would I need you for?" Seriously, Banks was more full of himself than usual today. "I can take care of both kids successfully and keep the house clean and keep my sanity."

Banks sputtered into the phone. "Do you even know how to change a diaper? Furthermore, are you aware of the consistency of toddler poo?"

Why had I called him again? "Look, I'll manage just fine. I'm sure it's not that difficult. Colby's just never been very good at..."

Banks cut me off. "So you haven't changed a diaper yet?"

I shifted uncomfortably on my feet. "No, not really."

"It's a yes-or-no question."

"I'm at work all day! And she just, you know…gets there faster."

"Ah, seems fair."

Guilt lodged in my throat. "Look, I'm working my ass off while she gets to stay home!"

Banks whistled under his breath, and then, "Say that again, only louder so every single parent in the office, mainly the female ones, can use you as target practice. I'll wait."

I rolled my eyes. "It's not what you think, they're good kids, they're—"

"Don't say it, don't say it, don't say it."

"Easy!"

"And there it is." I could hear him scrambling to his feet and pictured him pacing around his office. "Prepare yourself this morning, Rip, for this day, you go to war."

"You're exaggerating. Besides, how do you even know all of this? You're a bachelor!"

"My sister has seven children. I've been to hell and back, it's hot there, bro, very hot. Know that I do have a few personal days lined up. So if you find yourself in over your head with a need to prove the dear lady friend you refuse to admit you're attracted to despite the hate that festers between you wrong—give me a call."

The denial was on my tongue, but I couldn't get it out, why couldn't I get it out? "Whatever you say, man."

"Dude, you need me, more than you realize. All right, off to save the world. Mr. Stick, do send me text updates, preferably with video evidence."

"Stick?"

"Well, Stick Up Your Ass was just too long to say, you know? Didn't exactly flow."

"And Stick does?"

The line went dead right after more laughter on his end. I set my phone down on my dresser and stared into the mirror hanging on the wall above. Damn, I looked exhausted already.

Shaking the negative thoughts from my head, I started to get dressed for battle. For *working at home*. Damn it, Banks had put me off my game.

And he was exaggerating as per usual.

How hard could taking care of two little kids—one of whom was in school most of the day—really be?

Colby was struggling, sure. But she was just...not lazy, but...not used to following a schedule. Order. Organization. *Rules*.

These were things I excelled in. Just like I would excel in this new arrangement. It wasn't that hard. She just needed someone to show her how it was done.

And that someone was me.

She was going to come home to the house sparkling like a motherfucking diamond.

I'd be sitting on the sofa reading to both kids as they cuddled next to me—I'd have a glass of whisky in one hand and a cigar in the other, you know, if I smoked, which I wouldn't around kids, and she'd take in the roaring fire and clean kitchen and utter the magic words:

You. Were. Right.

Ha, now I really couldn't wait.

I quickly grabbed a pair of worn jeans that would be comfortable but wash easily, just in case I had a situation with the finger paints, which, as far as I could tell, were Viera's favorite and also the messiest thing on Earth, then grabbed a black T-shirt and put on my Rolex.

Whistling, I made my way down the stairs as the familiar smell of burning pancakes filled the air.

Ah, home sweet home.

"OK! Uncle Rip is here, kiddos. Auntie Colby's going to work!" Colby spun around at the sound of my voice. Her hair was pulled back into a neatly coiled braid, showing off her beautiful jawline, and she was wearing a white sundress with yellow heels that accentuated her hips and what the hell was I doing staring at her?

"Uh, um." I scratched my head. "My friend Banks will be there if you need anything, or you know, you could always"—I gulped and stared at her hips again—"text me or something or whatever." What the hell was wrong with my voice? "Coffee," I muttered to myself. "I just need coffee."

"Oh, we're out!" Colby shrugged a shoulder. "Maybe make a list of what we need at the grocery store, you know, since you love organizing so much!"

Out of coffee?

How did you run out of coffee?

And did that mean I had to grocery shop? With a toddler? Was that even physically possible?

"B-but—" I had barely gotten the word out when Ben threw his body against mine, his little arms coming around my hips. "We're going to be late for preschool!"

"Preschool," I repeated. "Right, school." I tripped over his backpack in an effort to get my shoes.

"Viera's been changed." Colby grabbed her purse and flowery monstrosity of a laptop bag. "Make sure you buckle her into the right car seat. Ben likes to sit in his old one on the passenger side. Don't let him convince you to swap it with the left seat, because the sun gets in Viera's eyes. Oh, and you have snack tomorrow, so make sure to get a final head count for the cupcakes we have to make later and get an up-to-date list of the classroom allergies so you don't make something that sends a kid to the hospital—"

"Make them?" I sputtered. "Why the hell am I making cupcakes when I can just buy them?"

"Good question. Solid one. Asked the same thing. I've now been uninvited to mommy happy hour for being so insensitive to the need to provide healthy, tasty food that won't, you know, *kill* anyone. Nut-free. Dairy-free. Soy-free—basically you're going to need to use chickpeas. I looked it up."

"Chick-*what*? Isn't that a bean?" I stepped through a Lego minefield and picked up Viera from the blue chair. "And why was Viera in trouble?"

"She broke two of my *Star Wars* Lego sets! On purpose!" Ben said in complete outrage. "And they were my favorite."

"Viera, why did you break his Lego sets?"

Over by the door, Colby started waving her hands like a windmill as Viera's big blue eyes met mine.

The lower lip trembled.

Oh shit.

"Honey, no, no, no, you're fine, don't cry." I patted her on the back just as the front door closed.

78

The hell?

"Did Colby just...leave?" I asked the universe and the two children I had to keep alive for the next few hours while starved of caffeine.

"She left a note!" Ben grabbed the yellow sticky note and frowned. "'Suck-er.' Hey, isn't that a lollipop? Are we getting candy for dinner?"

"I like suckers!" Viera stopped crying immediately. "Suckers, suckers, suckers." And now the kids were basically chanting.

I glared at the door Colby had just used as her exit and found myself slowly smiling.

I was the sucker?

She had to put up with Banks's constant interruptions. Good luck to her trying to hit her deadlines.

We'll see who's the sucker at the end of the day.

I pulled out my phone and typed in *chickpea cupcakes.*

"Bring it," I whispered. A challenge to the universe.

NINE

Colby

I was giddy on my way to Rip's office, which was surprising, really, since the last and only other time I'd been there I'd ended up in tears. I'd gone there to meet Monica and ended up eavesdropping on her and Rip discussing our one and only disastrous date.

I got there just in time to hear him tell her that I needed to grow the hell up rather than complain about the stress of my job. And that I needed to act like an actual adult rather than traveling all over the world. He said a few more hurtful things—private things I'd told him in confidence since he'd asked, and while it didn't matter that Monica knew, it hurt that he had such venom behind his words.

I pulled Rip's Mercedes into the first parking spot I could find and grinned. He'd never given me permission to take his car, but he needed the minivan to cart the kids around.

I cut the engine and grabbed my stuff. The office building was nestled right between a bagel shop, yay, and a coffee shop, double yay. Somehow, knowing that I had coffee and he was out added extra pep to my step as I opened the door to Rip's office building.

My joy was short lived. The woman who shall not be named greeted me with a cold stare. "Can I help you?"

I hesitated a bit, taking in yet another gorgeous pantsuit, this time black. Her earrings were gorgeous gold dangly things that would look ridiculous on me but kissed her shoulders in a way that screamed *rich*.

Which had always been the problem growing up. I was the kid who had zero parent involvement, who wore hand-me-downs until Monica finally took pity on me and gave me some of her clothes so I wouldn't get made fun of.

And it had just sucked.

All of it had sucked.

There had been no reason for Heather to pick on me apart from the fact that I was Monica's best friend and that meant I got to hang out with Rip, who was everyone's dream guy. Captain of basically everything, total heartthrob, straight-A-student Rip whose house I got to have sleepovers at.

I still remember the day Heather tripped me in gym, forcing me to land right at Rip's feet. I had a purple eye for a week.

I shot her a fake smile that I hoped looked at least a little genuine and bypassed her tidy mahogany desk like a woman on a mission. "I'm good, thanks."

Since Rip owned the firm, his office was huge and in the very back at the end of the hall.

I'd have peace.

Quiet.

A few minutes of sanity, even though I knew I would miss the kids because although it was stressful, they were ours, they were family, and seeing them reminded me of all those small moments that mattered, moments that you sometimes don't cherish enough because you always assume they'll be there.

At least I wouldn't have constant distractions, which always derailed my writing. Even if I got in the zone, all it took was one interruption to pull me out of it, no matter how cute the interruption.

Two hours, zero disruptions, and three cups of coffee later and I felt like a new woman.

I'd already finished two of my articles and sent ideas

to my boss for more content by noon. She'd been pretty understanding, but the blog she ran needed content, and the main part of my job was to bring that content at least three times a week, which before kids hadn't been a huge deal. Now I was ready to open a bottle of wine for finishing a sentence.

I mentally patted myself on the back. Unfortunately, my self-congratulatory moment was short lived. "You're not my cranky friend, Rip. Gotta admit, I like the view in here today way better. Smart woman with a pencil behind her ear, and what is that? A sundress? Let me guess, you purposely wear bright colors in hopes of giving Rip a heart attack?"

I gaped at the man standing in the doorway.

I couldn't help it.

He was drop-dead gorgeous in a slap-you-in-the-face sort of way that had you wanting to rub your eyes just to make sure you weren't hallucinating or, you know, dead.

The navy-blue suit he wore fit like it was custom tailored, and the top few buttons of his white shirt were undone, revealing a tan, firm chest. I could have sworn that he growled as he stalked toward the desk.

His hair fell in luscious, light-brown, messy waves that somehow managed to also look perfectly styled.

Green eyes crinkled in amusement as he leaned his muscled body over the desk and said, "Tell me everything."

"Huh?" *Stop drooling, Colby! Is this the part where he throws all the contents of the desk onto the ground and whispers, "Take me, I'm yours"? No? And where the hell is the signup sheet for that sort of office experience?*

"I said tell me everything, leave out no details. Just allow bathroom breaks and popcorn, because I have a feeling I'm going to be extremely entertained, and we can't have my blood sugar dropping too much if you're one of those people like Rip that takes about ten years to actually finish a story..." He finally took a breath. "I'll sit."

"The story...," I repeated with an embarrassed smile. "To a stranger? And what story? How it's going with a painfully anal individual under one roof with two kids—"

"I want to know how you got a few days off from mommy duty and managed to get Rip to agree to take care of the kids, because that's pretty much like witnessing a damn miracle." He took a breath before continuing. "He straightens his pencils...and now he's home with a three-year-old doing God knows what...please tell me you have a nanny cam so we can spy on the chaos."

"You talk a lot." I frowned.

"Yes." He nodded slowly. "Because if I don't, I'll die of boredom—you do realize this is an accounting firm, right? Do you even understand how boring it is? I've resorted to making up stories about the squirrels outside my window—they're expecting, by the way."

"Expecting what?"

"Puppies," he deadpanned. "What do you think?"

I snorted out a laugh. "How would you even know?"

"Was a vet in the past life." He snapped his fingers impatiently. "Now back to Rip. How did it go down?"

I sighed and closed my laptop. "Ten minutes, and then I need to get back to work."

"Fifteen."

"Twelve."

His smile was wicked. "Deal." He held out his hand. "I'm Banks, by the way, best friend to the anal man who normally occupies that desk and all-around cheerleader for Team Colby."

"Well, in that case." I grinned and leaned forward.

During the story of how Rip and I had come to switch places this week, he interrupted me about a million times and had to use the restroom twice, and by the time I was done, we'd been talking over an hour—or I'd been talking, he'd been interrupting. At least about halfway in, I finally got some of the story of how he'd ended up working with Rip and how they'd become the unlikeliest of friends, which of course made my stomach clench when I thought about Brooks and the bromance he and Rip had shared.

"Wow," Banks said after a few beats of miraculous silence. "He must really like you, or you are a master negotiator. Which, come to think of it, I've seen evidence of when you agreed to tell me the story..."

I rolled my eyes. "I highly doubt Rip likes me. He barely tolerates me. I pretty much drive him to drink on a daily basis, and I dared to order McDonald's, so..."

"He choked on a fry when he was sixteen, then puked up fries when he was drunk off his ass after a frat party. Hasn't been able to look at them again without wanting to die a little." He shrugged like the stories weren't a big deal. "This is why you both need me."

I raised an eyebrow. "We do?"

"Yeah, because that's the type of shit Rip would never admit to, his past indiscretions, failures, imperfections. On the outside all you see is a robot going through the motions, but he actually does know how to have fun. And he wasn't always this...controlled." His face flickered as he looked down at his hands briefly. What did he know that I didn't? I'd been in Rip's life whether he liked it or not for years.

"Well, I've never seen that side of him," I admitted finally. "Only the know-it-all side or the side that still holds our one horrific date over my head as if he had nothing to do with how bad the night went."

Banks's smile grew to epic proportions. "I forgot..." He wagged a finger at me. "You're the sneak kisser."

I groaned and contemplated throwing my body against the window in hopes of escape. I still felt embarrassed when I thought back on that moment, his face, my misreading of the situation.

"In my defense, I'd been nervous, had a bit too much to drink, and—wait, why am I defending myself to you? I barely know you! For all I know you could be lying about the best-friend thing. Then again, he did warn me about you before I left, yelling something about some man-whore in his office who has too much time on his hands." Honestly it was a bit of a blur considering I was so excited to leave the house and get some work done—not that I wanted to actually leave the kids, which ended up being the hard part. I wanted to leave and yet I didn't. And I still weirdly missed the chaos they brought to my day.

"Classic Rip." He laughed. "But really, Rip doesn't need someone to *like* him, he needs someone to *push* him. That's my role here at the office and apparently your role at home. I mean, if I was a chick or into dudes I'd be perfect for him!"

I choked on a laugh. "Can't wait to tell him you think you'd be a good husband."

"I'm more like his work husband." He grinned. "I make sure he eats lunch, takes breaks, and doesn't yell at people just because they wore red."

"He hates red," I admitted.

"Fucking hates it," he agreed. A soft chuckle slipped out. "He's a weird one, our Rip."

I nodded. "Now let me get back to work—" I opened my laptop and waited for him to leave.

Instead he put his feet up on Rip's desk. "Nah, I'm good."

"Banks!"

"Yes?"

"I need to work!"

"I know."

"You're distracting."

His shit-eating grin widened. "It's the face, isn't it?"

I had opened my mouth to respond when my cell phone rang, and I checked the screen. "It's Rip." I picked it up.

"Speakerphone this shit. Or hell, ask if he can

FaceTime!" Banks was suddenly right behind me, watching, listening, and damn he smelled good.

Focus, Colby

"Hey, what's up?" I tapped the speakerphone button and waited.

Viera was bawling in the background, and from the rattles and clanks, it sounded like he was at the store. Yay, we'd have groceries! I might be annoyed with him, but I was so thrilled he'd actually attempted the impossible I could kiss him.

"I can't find the damn chickpeas. What the hell is a chickpea? The recipe said I needed two cans, and some organic coconut flour, and—Viera, hey, hey, hey, the big bird didn't mean it, all right? Just calm down—"

"Never tell a woman to calm down," Banks said under his breath. "That's like Manhood 101."

"Are you with a guy?" Rip asked.

"I wouldn't necessarily call him a guy," I joked, earning a glare from Banks, who decided to join in on the convo.

"Hey, man!" His smile was one of pure joy. "You, uh, you doing OK? Want some of that help I offered this morning?"

"I'm good. Everything's fine! Viera, the bird was

sad, OK? That's why it flew down so close to you, and it didn't follow us into the grocery store, OK?"

"But it be there when we go back outside!" she wailed.

Banks whistled. "Kid really doesn't like birds, does she?"

"You have no idea." I sighed as Rip made a strangled cough in the background, then the line went dead.

"I think he's doing fantastic, you?" Banks's smug grin actually had me smiling back at him. "Honest moment, you like that he's struggling and so do I. He needs a bit of mess in his life." He eyed me up and down like he was waiting for me to acknowledge that I was, in fact, the mess he was referring to.

I cleared my throat. "I'm not a mess."

Wow, even I didn't believe me. Great.

"Sure. OK." He drummed his fingertips against Rip's desk. How were even his hands attractive? "I never said being disorganized was a bad thing. I like messes. But more importantly, my point is you'd be good for him, and because we're friends now—"

I tilted my head to the left and subjected him to an assessing stare. "Are we, though?"

"I'm going to help you."

"Help me what?"

"Win him over. Get him to give you some slack."

"Ha!" I crossed my arms. "It's impossible. I've tried."

So damn much it was almost embarrassing. I did everything in my power to make him see me as an equal and always came up short, which just irritated me more because I knew my worth—the problem was, he didn't, and he never would. He wasn't the type to see my accomplishments, only my failures, and it sucked because I truly did want his respect. I wanted so much more than that, truthfully, but I'd given up on that a long time ago.

"Guys like Rip need a different approach. If you turn into his perfect woman, you're going to turn into him, and he's going to be bored to tears. He just needs someone who can force him to acknowledge his attraction to you."

Wait. What? We had been talking about Rip being appreciative of me. Not being attracted to me! "He's not—"

"Unless he's blind," Banks interrupted, "he is. Quick question, were you two sexting yesterday? Around ten a.m.?"

My cheeks heated. "More like hate texting."

"Hate texting." He shrugged. "Sexting." Another shrug. "It's really the same thing, you know that, right?"

I rolled my eyes despite my sudden excitement that Banks somehow knew that Rip and I had been texting. And having fun while doing it. Had Banks walked in on Rip staring at his phone? Had Rip told him he was enjoying our conversation?

Ugh, now I was daydreaming again about the guy who thought I had the maturity of a preschooler. Great.

"Actually we weren't even hate texting," I announced. "It was more like threat texting."

"He was smiling," Banks said triumphantly. "Down at his phone, with a giant grin on his face that I haven't seen in forever. Plus, he's not really a texter, comes across as a giant jackass when he uses the written word, doesn't know how to cut things up with an emoji or funny meme. Hell, he even uses proper grammar; would it kill him to use a contraction?"

"And corrects others' grammar, don't forget that." But even as I said it, my heart was lodged in my throat, my pulse quickening. Was it true? Could Rip actually ...like me?

The last thing I needed was an awkward situation between me and Rip, though. I immediately deflated. Getting my hopes up was so not the way to make things less awkward with the guy I was raising two kids with.

This conversation with Banks was just confusing

me even more. I didn't want Banks to be right. I didn't want to hope. All hope did was make me think there was a chance something was there, a something I'd always wanted, and I wasn't rested enough or emotionally stable enough right now to take rejection from the man who was sleeping just down the hall from me.

I shook my head as if to say, *No, no, I can't have this conversation.*

Banks rested a hand on mine. "Nope, no giving up before we even start plotting world domination or, you know, Rip domination. Now, steak or Italian?"

The guy was exhausting; beautiful, but exhausting. "Why?"

"Answer the question."

"Italian?"

"Great, I'll pick you up around nine. Bedtime is around eight thirty, correct?"

"Wait, what do you mean you're picking me up?" I asked, suddenly confused.

"We're going to start dating." He winked. "But don't worry. I won't fall in love with you. It's really hard for guys like me to catch feelings."

"Wh-why are we dating again?" My head spun along with the room. How would pretending to date Banks even work?

Rip would probably shove me out the door and tell me to have a good time just to get me out of the house—OK, maybe not that harsh, but he wouldn't be jealous; he'd have to actually like me to be jealous. So he'd smiled at our text conversation. So what? I refused to believe that meant he wanted to date me and would be mad if Banks did. I wasn't stupid.

Banks winked. "Because guys like Rip react to one thing and one thing only." He got up and started walking toward the door before calling over his shoulder, "Competition."

I fell back against my chair. "But—"

"Wear black. See you later, beautiful."

"What the heck just happened?" I whispered to myself. At least I'd get Italian out of the deal and dinner with a hot guy, so really there was no loss there, but his plan just seemed like a way to get me out to dinner or maybe even get in my pants.

Huh, there was a thought.

Sex.

With a guy who actually liked me, or at least seemed to.

If Banks thought it would work, it was either one or the other: he wanted to go out with me, which was great, or he truly knew Rip well enough that he thought this would catch his attention.

Hope: there it was again.

I guessed I had nothing to lose.

Nothing at all.

Only gains at this point. A night out would be nice.

I found myself smiling despite the fact that my heart reminded me I'd much rather have a do-over with Rip—different restaurant, same situation—where he didn't scold me or scowl, where he genuinely liked me, and where he returned a kiss with the desperation I felt every time I looked his way and his eyes went dead.

Thankfully, I didn't see Banks the rest of the afternoon.

More importantly, I made good headway on my article about fish and chips in the UK and the best places to visit in London. Thankfully, the blog I worked for knew the entire situation I was dealing with and had said I could do a series of articles about my favorite places I'd visited in the last two years and the places I wanted to visit in the future, which meant a bit more research, but it was something, and I was still getting paid, which was huge.

God, I missed traveling.

It wasn't even about the food or the articles, it was the different cultures, the different experiences. While Rip might not think it was a real job, it fit me well because it was constantly changing, constantly interesting. I could never have a desk job—ever. So while he didn't understand my work, I really didn't understand his either. I would have died of boredom.

A sudden knock on the door jolted me out of my thoughts.

"Banks, if you interrupt me again..." I groaned and looked up into Heather's bright-green eyes.

Her face was impassive.

Was she even breathing?

Was she even human?

And how tall were those heels? They were red and looked like weapons.

Maybe she had changed, we could become best friends, and she'd let me borrow them. Even if I was just walking around the house with a glass of wine, I'd at least feel fancy.

I deflated a bit; I was being ridiculous. People change, clearly. I wasn't the same person I'd been in high school, thank God. Maybe I needed to give her a chance. It wasn't like she'd been rude to me; cool, but not rude.

"Hi! Can I help you?" I tried to sound sweet, when I really wanted to run out of the room screaming in fear that she was seconds away from embarrassing me or saying something cruel.

There was no way she didn't remember me, right?

No. Way.

I waited for her to say something.

"I remember you now." Her smile didn't reach her eyes, and I hated that it took me back to a dark place when I was here to actually get things done and focus. "We went to high school together, didn't we?"

"Yup." I quickly gathered my things and forced another smile. "I figured it was just so long ago you didn't remember. No worries. I gotta get going back to the kids, though, it's been an adjustment, as you know."

She was blocking the door, her eyes drinking me in, not in a nasty way but more of a curious way. "He's mine, you know."

"Banks?" I laughed, suddenly realizing that despite how good-looking Banks was, I wasn't at all interested. "You can have him."

"Not Banks." She said it like a fact, like a fact I should know. Two plus two equals four. Not Banks but Rip, it had to be.

"Well?" I shrugged lightly. "You're welcome to him

too. I'm just trying to survive ketchup stains, the PTA, and potty training."

"I can see that," she said with a sudden smile. "Sorry, I just wanted to be clear. I've been interested in Rip awhile. But you know men, they're clueless." She literally flipped her hair like an actress in a bad soap opera. "Anyway, Rip and I make sense, and it felt like he was finally seeing it after our date. But then everything slipped into chaos with the kids, and I know it's been a rough adjustment, especially for someone like him." She shot me a bright smile. "He'll come to his senses. You know, if he could get any free time instead of playing pretend dad." She laughed.

I almost punched her. How insensitive could she be? And how insecure could I be that I was staring her down like she was somehow the perfect person for him when she seemed just as selfish as she'd been in high school?

Old me would have been grumpy and rubbed it in Rip's face that of course he deserved someone just as arrogant. New me? I kind of wanted to stand in front of him, the kids, the cat, and tell her to back the hell off.

Honestly, she'd be perfect for him, or at least the old him who didn't have kids and preferred everything perfect. "I really do need to get going."

"Oh, sure." She moved out of the way, her smile wide. "Will Rip be at the office tomorrow?" I frowned. If they were dating, wouldn't he have told her that? Her eyes flickered away briefly. "My phone's been acting up, so my texts keep bouncing back, otherwise I'm sure he would have let me know..."

She cleared her throat and looked away. Ten bucks said she was lying, but I had no proof other than the way she refused to make eye contact.

It was my turn to offer a smug smile. "No, actually. You get me all week! I'm sure he'll get back to you, right? In the meantime get that phone taken care of, yeah?"

Her smile fell and then, "Sure, of course!"

"Great! Have a good night!"

I know it's wrong and bad and yay women support-ing women, but I did feel a sense of excitement and maybe a tiny rush wash over me as I skipped toward Rip's car and got into it. My high school self was preen-ing while my adult self told me to calm down and try not to back up into another car or a tree. I started it just fine and pulled out of the parking lot, then gave her a little wave as I left and made my way toward the house.

It was probably the first time in my life that I'd felt like I had something over Heather Donnelly.

Let her be gorgeous and tall.

But right now?

I was driving her crush's car.

And there was nothing she could do about it but stare and wonder what would happen when I went home to him.

I actually laughed out loud. Yeah, clearly it had been a long day, because the joke was on me since the minute I got there it would be like hell had been unleashed in that place. Actually I was betting on it and needed it to be like that. If he had laminated schedules on the fridge and baked homemade cupcakes in advance just to test out his recipe—I was going to murder him.

I clenched the steering wheel and mulled over the whole Heather situation and the fact that Banks wanted to fake date me to make Rip jealous. Frowning, I took the corner and waited at the stoplight. Why would Banks suggest something like that if Rip was actually interested in Heather? Unless Banks was right and Rip did have feelings for me, and she was lying? The entire conversation with her was suspicious.

Suddenly Banks's idea didn't seem so horrible. I'd pined after Rip for half my adult life. If I didn't try to see if those feelings were reciprocated now, then when?

As I pulled Rip's Benz into our subdivision and

then into our driveway, I willed the universe to show me a sign that he was struggling with the kids and needed help. Come on, where was an SOS when you needed one? It's not that I wanted him to fail, I just wanted him to see what it was like to be in over your head and want to day drink in the pantry. Was that really too much to ask?

Damn. The house looked normal.

Rip wasn't outside crying.

Ben wasn't setting Stu on fire.

And Viera wasn't wailing about birds.

Hmmmmm.

I pulled into the driveway and grabbed my things, then slowly walked toward the door, pressing my ear against it to listen for the sound of chaos inside.

Only there was no chaos.

No screaming, just the background noise of the nightly news.

"What are you doing?" neighbor Mrs. Harris called loudly. "Do I need to call the police?"

This woman.

"No, Mrs. Harris!" I waved. "Just checking something—"

The door swung open.

Rip stood there wearing a perfectly clean white

shirt. Odd. Black sweatpants and honest-to-God black-rimmed glasses that literally brought every hot-nerd fantasy I'd ever had to life.

"You just going to spy on me or actually come in?" His eyes narrowed.

Then my eyes narrowed.

His narrowed further.

"I'm suspicious," I said, walking in after him, not staring at his perfect body as he gave me his delicious back and walked into the kitchen. "Something smells good!"

"I cooked." He said it so simply I wanted to smack him across the face with the nearest blunt object. "Followed some casserole recipe."

"Of course you did." I set my things on the kitchen counter, my eyes taking in the mostly clean living room and kitchen.

Other than a few dishes in the sink, everything looked perfect. As if Rip had balanced stay-at-home-dad life like a pro.

Still not trusting it, I walked over to the fridge.

It was full.

Just as I was about to admit semidefeat, something caught my eye. "What's that?"

"What's what?" He crossed his arms.

"That coming out of the pantry?" I pointed again at part of what looked like a flag poking out from under the pantry door.

I went over to open it, only to have Rip sprint ahead of me and cover the door with his massive body. "Don't."

"Got something to hide...Rip?"

His eyes fell to my lips before he responded, "No."

"Let me in the pantry."

"No."

"Rip!" I reached out to grab the handle, but he put his hands on my shoulders and tried to steer me away.

There was no way I could outmaneuver him, so I was about to go slack in his arms and make a run for it when Ben came running around the corner and announced, "Uncle Rip cried today!"

I stilled in his arms.

Rip swore under his breath.

"Swear jar!" Ben yelled.

"Oh?" I kept my laugh in. My smile, however, was huge. "What happened?"

"I think he's stressed," Ben whispered loudly.

"Ben." Rip gritted his teeth. "Remember what we talked about."

"Oh, sorry, yeah, don't tell Aunt Colby you got stressed, and don't tell Aunt Colby you ordered food."

"Son of a bitch," he swore again.

"Ahem, swear jar." I elbowed him in the ribs.

"I could have bankrolled Ben's college with the amount of swearing that took place under this roof today—I'm not proud of it." Rip ran a hand through his gorgeous hair. "This is the fourth shirt I've put on today."

"It's nice." I chewed my lower lip and stared into his green eyes. "Did you maybe want me to help you with something now that I'm home?"

His right eye twitched, and then he opened the pantry door and showed me his shame.

Sweet mother of God, miracles did happen. Toys. Clothes. DoorDash bags, groceries that still hadn't been put away, and Stu...oh crap. "How long has the cat been in—"

"Shit." Rip was on a roll today! "Ben, get your damn cat out of the pantry and clean up his poop!"

"Stu's Viera's cat!" Ben argued as he came over toward us, and then he started gagging. "I can't!"

And just like that, the peaceful house exploded as Viera ran down the stairs with a princess dress on and my makeup all over her face.

Mainly red lipstick.

THE GODPARENT TRAP

"It looks like she murdered someone," Rip said under his breath.

"It's terrifying," I agreed. "Why don't you go take care of Carrie, and I'll take care of this and the poop."

Words I never thought I would ever utter, but here we were!

Rip's attention jerked to me. "You aren't going to fight for makeup removal duty?"

I just shrugged. "You were in chaos all day. I'll deal with the poop, you deal with our future murderer."

His lips twitched.

Our eyes locked for one small moment.

And then the moment was broken by the cat making this screaming noise as Ben picked him up by his front legs.

"Honey, honey, no, no, we don't hold Stu that way, it makes the kitty sad."

"No, he likes it!" Ben argued, and then he sprinted away. "Look, he's meowing!"

"Godspeed." Rip put a hand on my shoulder.

I gaped. "Did you just crack a joke?"

"Never." He winked.

Actually winked.

I tried not to let air get caught in my throat, just like

I tried not to read into any of it, which was basically impossible. But before I could say anything, he was carrying Viera upstairs. And while I wrangled a cat, cleaned up poop, and helped Ben put away groceries, my heart held out a little bit more hope that maybe...

Maybe we were going to be OK.

TEN

Rip

She didn't see the beads of sweat running down my back.

Or hear the panic in my head when I saw her slowly roll up to the house in my car as if she were casing the joint.

I'd had to ask a five-year-old how to download a food delivery app—and I'd had to leave the grocery store twice so I could go to the van and grab Bugsy and a forgotten shoe that Viera had somehow thrown off during our drive.

I also had to scream, "No, birds, no," so Viera would feel better when we walked back outside to load up the van, meaning I got so distracted I still don't know how the eggs didn't make it home. I blame the birds.

I was humbled—to say the least.

And I would rather die than admit that to Colby, but something had shifted today. It felt like we'd called a truce, which was unexpected and felt...right while at the same time feeling wrong because this wasn't the life we were supposed to have. The kids were supposed to have the best life. The perfect life. Two parents who loved each other.

Not us.

Never us.

It was like Colby and I had found solidarity through the chaos. We were a team. Connected by love for these kids and panic over our inadequacies and...something else that I really didn't want to think about.

After helping Viera get what seemed like two tubes of red lipstick off her still-stained-red face, Colby and I continued to divide and conquer.

By the time the kids were in bed—earlier than we'd ever been able to get them down before—I was ready for a bottle of whisky and a two-day nap.

Instead I poured both myself and Colby a glass of wine and went into the living room.

She appeared fifteen minutes later wearing a short black cocktail dress that hugged her every curve. Wait. What?

Was she dressed up for me?

"I have a date," she announced.

I choked on my next sip of wine. "What?"

"A date." She beamed. "You know, where someone buys you dinner or drinks or even just coffee. You share riveting conversation and, if things go well, a kiss..."

My stomach sank. "How did you even have time to find a date?"

"Oh." Her smile was utter perfection, like sunshine and warmth and everything I'd been missing since my sister's death. "He found me."

The hell?

I took another slow, tentative sip of wine and narrowed my eyes. "Didn't you go to the office today?"

"Yeah." She grabbed a small silver clutch and dropped her cell phone into it. "I figured that it would be OK since it was after bedtime."

I was still gaping when the doorbell rang.

My brain told me to yank open the door, tell the bastard to leave, then camp out in the front yard with a six-pack of beer and a lawn chair just in case he got any ideas about coming back.

What the hell was wrong with me?

Slowly I walked over to the door and opened it wide. "You."

"Me." Banks smiled. "Can I come in?" He didn't let me answer as he moved past me and toward Colby.

"You look beautiful." He leaned in and kissed her on the cheek, and the fucker lingered.

What the hell?

I clenched my fists as he reached for her wine and took a sip.

"That's Colby's," I found myself saying.

Banks narrowed his eyes at me, his smile knowing. "Enjoying a glass of wine together after a long day? How cozy."

I was going to kill him. What the hell was he pulling? Was this a joke?

"Here." Banks handed Colby the glass. "Take a few sips for liquid courage—I don't drive slow—actually I don't do anything slow."

"Don't you have a girlfriend?" I blurted while Colby took a few sips, then set the glass back down.

"Who?" Banks looked around the room. "Me?" He laughed. "You know I don't do girlfriends...or should I say I never used to, and then this woman walked into my life, and, well, I think it may be time to rethink my life's plan. The heart wants what it wants, you know?"

"No," I grumbled. "I don't."

Colby's face fell, which made zero sense because she didn't feel anything toward me. At least not since our one disastrous date.

Right?

Right?

Tears pooled in her eyes

Fuck.

I'd just hurt her feelings. Monica always said I was the most obtuse guy around.

Shit.

I tried fixing it. "No, that's not what I mean, I meant—"

"Well?" Banks reached for Colby's hand, completely ignoring me. "Let's go, we have reservations." As he walked past me he whispered under his breath, "I wouldn't wait up."

Before I could even mutter, *What the hell*, they were gone. I grabbed the other full glass of wine and stared at it in disbelief.

She wanted to go out on a date with Banks?

Banks was a complete player with absolutely no shame. Was he going to hit on her? Should I text her?

Warn her?

And why was she all dressed up?

She'd looked good.

Happy.

She never smiled at me like that. I'd had her rage, her annoyance, I'd had it all, but this? This was new territory. A territory I was suddenly angry someone else had discovered.

A pang of jealousy shot through my chest as I swiped my phone from the counter and sent off a text.

Me:

> You know he'll sleep with anything, right?

Colby:

> …was that supposed to be a warning or an insult or both?

Me:

> A warning! He'll use his moves on you. Whatever you do, don't let him tell you the story of the time he went camping.

Colby:

> I should be worried about the camping story. Gotcha. Can I enjoy my date now?

Beads of sweat formed on my forehead and rolled down my back.

Me:

> Don't stay out too late. The kids will be upset if they wake up and don't see you.

THE GODPARENT TRAP

I was being ridiculous.

I was overreacting.

I stared at my phone, willing her to text me back.

Finally the little bubbles popped up on the screen.

Colby:

> Stop texting my date, man, that's bad form. Don't worry, I'll have her back by eleven. Just don't wait up. I don't need an audience when I kiss her good night. Byeeeeee

Kiss?

He was being sarcastic.

Right?

I clutched my phone so hard that I was afraid I was going to split the screen in two. Then I grabbed the bottle of wine, poured another glass, and waited in the dark like the proverbial overprotective father waiting for his daughter to come home from prom.

I fell asleep waiting but shot up off the couch the minute the front door opened, revealing Colby, sans heels, tiptoeing through the kitchen.

"It's midnight," I grumbled.

"Ouch!" Colby banged her hip into the countertop and turned toward me, her eyes lit with laughter like she'd just had the time of her life while all I'd gotten was a kink in my neck from sleeping on the couch. "Where did that countertop come from?"

"Are you drunk?" I hissed.

She glared. "No, just clumsy, but thanks."

I rocked back on my heels, then shoved my hands into my pockets. "What happened to eleven?"

"Oh." She tossed her clutch onto the chair next to me and then leaned against it. "We were back at eleven, we just got to talking..."

My ears perked up. "You had that much to talk about with Banks?"

"He's a talker." She smiled again.

Why was she smiling?

Was it because they had been doing more than talking?

Was Banks really that charming?

My eyes narrowed.

She frowned at me. "You look like you're about to give me a lecture."

Probably because I was—and I'd opened my mouth to do just that when Viera's voice called out, "I puked!" Sobbing hiccups followed.

Colby was up the stairs in seconds, and I wasn't far behind her. She scooped up Viera and carried her into the bathroom, where Viera had narrowly missed her target of the toilet and hit part of the shower curtain and the rug.

Tears streamed down her face as she leaned against Colby, her face blotchy. "I want my mommy!"

My stomach thudded to the ground, and my heart followed as Colby held Viera close, ruining her dress with tears and puke. "I do too, honey, I do too."

I hadn't expected her to say that.

I'd expected her to say something more logical, like, *But your mom's not here, we are, and I know that's hard but it's all you have.*

Instead she'd empathized with Viera, in a way that I wouldn't have but in a way that Viera 100 percent needed. She stopped sobbing and just held Colby close, her chubby fingers gripping at Colby like she was afraid she was going to disappear too.

"Rip." Colby's voice jolted me away from my thoughts. "Can you go grab some children's Tylenol? We'll need to alternate between that and ibuprofen every four hours...she's burning up."

Shocked, I could only stand there and gape. "How do you even know that? Should I look it up and double-check? Actually I can call urgent care and—"

"Just trust me on this, Rip. Please?" Colby's eyes filled with a look I couldn't read. "Last time Ben was sick I was staying the night and that's exactly what the pediatrician said to do when there's a fever."

"Sorry," I rasped. "I'm just..."

"I know." Colby gave me an already-exhausted smile that basically said neither of us was going to get any sleep that night.

I left them in the bathroom and had started walking down the hall when Ben stumbled out of his room, took one look at me, and hurled all over the floor.

I jerked back and nearly fell down the stairs as he wiped his mouth and mumbled, "S-sorry, Uncle Rip."

"Bud." I almost gagged. "It's fine, you're sick, does your head hurt?"

"Mmmmm." He swayed in front of me. "My body hurts."

"OK, buddy." I led him into the bathroom. "Let's get you cleaned up first, and then we'll get some medicine in you."

"What's wrong?" Colby looked over her shoulder. "Ben, are you OK?"

"He's sick too." I pulled his Spider-Man shirt over his head and tossed it on the floor, then grabbed a washcloth and wiped his mouth.

He seemed to be handling everything well, but then

he looked up at me with tears in his eyes. "I want my mom."

Taking a cue from Colby, I pulled him into my arms and whispered, "Me too, buddy. Me too."

He burst into tears, his skin hot against mine. Over his head, Colby and I shared a look of utter sadness.

Hopelessness soon followed.

And then Colby took charge, something I'd never seen, like some unknown maternal instinct switch had been flipped.

"Let's all go into your parents' old room while Uncle Rip grabs some medicine." She was already leading them both out of the bathroom while I quickly cleaned up the puke in both locations. I grabbed the medicine from the cabinet downstairs.

By the time I was back upstairs, at least ten minutes had passed, and both kids were sitting against the pillows in their parents' old bed, their eyes heavy.

"Uncle Rip." Viera yawned. "Will you come cuddle me?"

"I was just going to ask if I could." I smiled and held out the syringe of pink medicine. "Open up first."

She made a face, then swallowed the medicine.

"You're next, Ben." He took the medicine like a

champ and then curled up next to Colby, his head resting against her shoulder.

It wasn't supposed to be like this. How many nights had Brooks and Monica done exactly this? Lain down with their kids, cuddled them. And in any of those times had they ever thought that one day they'd just disappear?

With a sigh, I set the medicine down, ready to lie next to Viera, only to have her shake her head. "No, you needs to be in the middle, that's how we always laid in the bed."

Grief tugged at my heart as I crawled over her and then pulled her into my arms.

Colby sighed next to me as Ben clung to her. Soon both kids were asleep, and Colby and I were lying next to one another, staring up at the dimmed lights, sandwiched between the kids.

"It wasn't supposed to be like this," Colby whispered, reading my mind as I tried to fight back the tears that were always threatening, along with the tight feeling in my throat that refused to go away.

I knew the minute I grieved, it would make this real.

For weeks now I'd almost made myself believe that Monica and Brooks would walk back through that door. For once I wanted to be more like Colby, believing that we'd see them again someday, that there was a place for good people in the afterlife, and that they were together watching over us.

Finally I cleared my throat and answered, "I know."

"I miss them."

I didn't trust my voice, so instead of telling her I missed them too, I inched my hand across the duvet and grasped her fingertips.

She squeezed my hand back and held it until her breathing became heavy. I turned then, stealing a glance at this all-over-the-place woman who loved these kids with the same ferocity I did.

Colby was frowning in her sleep, her lips slightly parted as if even in her sleep she was ready to talk my ear off or argue. She made a funny noise and then let out a snore, ruining the moment, or maybe just making it more real.

This was my reality now.

Two kids.

A house in the suburbs.

And a confusing, chaotic woman whom I argued with daily. I almost laughed when I realized that was how the majority of people would describe marriage after ten years.

We'd just skipped a few steps, hadn't we?

ELEVEN

Colby

The kids were sick for two straight days, so instead of going into the office and working, I stayed home and helped Rip. Both of us were so exhausted by Friday that we weren't even arguing with each other anymore. We were just ships passing in the night, our only focus getting the kids better. We'd tuck them in their beds and then crawl into our own, only to find that kids are creatures of habit—which meant we'd been all four of us sleeping in the same bed for three straight nights.

I'd been sleeping in the smallest guest room after Rip had chosen the biggest one for himself, of course. And now...now the kids wanted us all together.

The new sleeping arrangements meant I'd been sleeping next to Rip for the last few nights. At first I'd tried to inch away from him, and then I'd realized that no matter how hard I tried to do just that, I always woke up with my face plastered against his neck, sometimes with drool coming out of my mouth.

This morning he just looked at his wet shoulder, then back up at me, then went back to sleep.

Exhaustion apparently made him less fastidious, like he didn't even have the energy to tell me to move or stop slobbering on him.

When Friday morning came, the kids' fevers had been gone for twenty-four hours and they were finally looking like themselves again. As much as I didn't want to leave them, I was excited to get back to the office and finish my next post, about Edinburgh. I was writing about all the best places to eat in Scotland, and I couldn't wait to dive into the research I hadn't been able to do when I'd been there two years before. I'd had another trip planned before the accident, but I'd had to cancel it, of course, and I honestly hadn't thought about it since.

All my thoughts these days were centered on the kids. And trying to figure out how the hell I was supposed to learn to be a mother overnight.

And getting along with Rip so we didn't add any more trauma to these already-traumatized kids.

"Don't forget that Ben has his jujitsu match today at four." I choked down the rest of my coffee, then groaned when I looked down and noticed that I'd spilled on the white wrap dress I was wearing.

Rip sighed. "Do you have a calm bone in your body?"

"No." I shrugged. "Not really." I grabbed his keys again.

"Wait." He rushed past Viera, who was already coloring her soon-to-be masterpiece. It looked like two demons haunting a smiley face, but she'd very proudly announced she was drawing us. It was low-key terrifying. "Aren't you going to change?"

I looked down. "No, I'll just put on a cardigan."

Rip and I groaned in unison as Viera started belting out "Cardigan" by Taylor Swift. I'd completely forgotten about the trigger word.

Once Viera started, it was hard to get her to stop.

Rip shot me a look of betrayal while I tried to hide my smile behind my hand. "Payback's a bitch," he said under his breath. "And why not just take the time to change real quick?"

I shrugged. "Why bother? I mean, I'm not at your office to impress anyone."

His eyebrows shot up. "Oh?"

I quickly recovered. "Banks likes me coffee stains and all!"

Rip's eyes narrowed. "He *like*-likes you?"

"Well, I haven't officially sent him a circle-yes-or-no note, but I have a strong feeling he'd put a heart next to the *yes* with a red pen," I said sarcastically.

Rip glared. "He's a player, he could be using you."

"Ooooh, let him use me away, then," I teased.

Rip's eyes narrowed further, and from the deep breath he took I could tell he was about to launch into another lecture. Thankfully, Ben chose that moment to speed around the corner and throw himself into Rip's arms. "I brushed my teeth for the whole 'Happy Birthday' song!"

"Good job, buddy!" Rip smiled, genuinely proud of Ben, and my heart did a little flip-flop as I watched them.

Good-looking men shouldn't be allowed to do things like hold babies or smile at kids, it just makes a woman's ovaries go, *It's time! Pick us!*

"Aunt Colby, why are you smiling like that?" Ben asked.

I probably looked possessed, my smile wide, my eyes even wider to drink in the scene in front of me. I recovered as quickly as possible and willed myself not to blush when Rip's gaze fell to mine. "Aunt Colby was probably thinking about her food apps again."

"Guilty." He looked delicious this morning. Seriously

delicious. Why wasn't Rip in an app? I'd go broke using all the extra coins or whatever they charged for his avatar just so I could stare at him—and I'd just made things super creepy.

"Gotta go." I bolted toward the door, nearly tripping in my heels, and narrowly survived a bunch of scattered Legos in the middle of the floor. "Love you guys!"

"Love you too!" Viera announced.

"Me too!" Ben yelled following Colby outside the house. "Uncle Rip, will you miss Colby?"

"Terribly," Rip said, voice tight like he was lying through his teeth.

"I'm leaving you the van." I forced a smile, then made a quick getaway, calling over my shoulder, "Your car can go really fast!"

"Colby!" Rip called after me. "You hit a mailbox just three weeks ago. Come back with any scratches on her and you'll be rubbing them out with a toothbrush!"

"Ewwwwww." Ben made a face and ran back into the house while Rip stood there, arms crossed, looking every bit the sexy accountant who saved people from their taxes like a damn hero.

"You must know a lot about rubbing one out," I said in an innocent voice.

Rip's jaw dropped, and I refrained from doing a happy dance, although the fact that I'd actually gotten a reaction out of him was cause for celebration. "I rarely have to...hey, what was the name of that vibrator Monica got you?"

"There are kids!" I roared.

"They're inside," he snapped back.

"Unattended," I pointed out as Mrs. Harris opened her front door, grabbed the paper, and then stood there, sipping her coffee like we were her morning entertainment.

"It was a male's name...let me think..." Rip tapped his chin with his fingertips. "The Duke of Hastings..." I sprinted away from the car, and before I knew what I was doing I was clapping a hand over that gorgeous and ridiculous mouth.

His eyes flashed as I very slowly pulled my hand away. "Tell one person, and I'm putting a pillow over your face once you fall asleep."

"I like pillows."

"You won't be alive to like this one, Rip."

"What, are you embarrassed?" He leaned down, his mouth inches from mine. "Don't be...we all have needs. Oh, and Colby, next time you try to win an argument, I'd remember this moment right here. But don't worry, you're practically family, this is a safe space, you know? You can have all the feelings you want, promise."

"Safe space my ass," I said through gritted teeth. "Now flash one of those sexy smiles over to Mrs. Harris so she doesn't think we've been arguing."

"Did you just call me sexy?" he said, ignoring my comment.

I tried like hell not to flinch. "It was a total accident, but yes. I'm desperate," I teased in a way that I hoped would shut down the situation. "So hurry up. I want her face flaming red and her brain thinking about taking out her dentures and going to town." Where did that even come from?

I blamed Banks.

Or maybe it was just exhaustion?

"You've single-handedly killed any future erections. You know that, right?"

Good. "Dentures, dentures, dentures. Hurry!"

Muttering a curse, he slowly turned his head and gave Mrs. Harris a little wave and then bam.

The smile.

Not a forced one.

Not the ones he grudgingly gave me.

But a holy-shit-I'm-selling-all-my-worldly-possessions-for-one-more smile.

Mrs. Harris clutched at her chest.

"I didn't say to give her a heart attack." I smacked him.

Slowly Mrs. Harris returned the smile and then blew him a kiss.

"Catch the kiss." I elbowed him.

"You catch it!"

"And I'm the immature one," I grumbled, reaching into thin air, stealing the kiss, and putting it on his cheek.

Mrs. Harris waved again and then continued to watch like a hawk while I awkwardly cleared my throat and pulled away from his warmth. "Yeah, so I'll just be getting back to the car..."

"Yes, and I'll just be inside with the kids...solving world hunger."

"Do that." I smiled. "But maybe work on their hunger first."

"I'm gonna make another pancake attempt."

"Keep the fire department number close, sweetheart." I was trying to make him uncomfortable again.

Instead he smiled. "I'm on it, boopkins!"

"That's the best you could come up with?" I rolled my eyes.

"I'm a guy. You're lucky I came up with a word at all." And with that he went inside.

RACHEL VAN DYKEN

Apparently I was the most boring human alive because the minute he was gone, Mrs. Harris bolted back into her house.

Shaking my head, I dropped behind the wheel and started the engine, then pulled out of the driveway, not even questioning why I was smiling so hard my face hurt.

Had Rip and I just had... a moment again?

I promised myself I wouldn't analyze it the entire drive to the office, and when Heather gave me a snooty look from the front desk, all I kept mentally saying was, *Ha, but did you talk about sex toys together? I think not!*

Banks was in Rip's office, clearly waiting for me. "You're still smiling." He lifted a coffee cup that read "Drink the Coffee, Be the Shit" to his mouth. "By my estimation that smile means you had a good morning with our friend Rip. He's still alive, and he hasn't put his foot in his mouth as per usual. BTW, has he asked you out during recess yet or are we still in the note-passing stage?"

"It's not like that." I tried to hide my frown. "And get out of my chair."

He spun around in a circle and then stood, towering over me.

I had a hard time swallowing as his eyes drank in every inch of me before he whispered, "Coffee stain."

Only he said it in such a gruff, sexy whisper that it didn't register until a few seconds later as I finally unstuck my feet from the floor and moved around him. "I was already nearly out the door, so I just grabbed a random cardigan."

Banks grinned. "Tell me Rip saw this entire scenario taking place in real time?"

"He wanted me to change."

"This may actually be the final thing that kills him. You know he'll obsess over this for the entire day, don't you?

I just grinned. "First off, he would never, second, why would I change just because he asked me to?"

"I'd give you a high five if I wasn't afraid of cooties."

I laughed. "Yeah, well, one day you'll grow up and actually like girls, Banks."

"Women." He took another sip of his coffee. "I like women." He moved to sit in one of the chairs and then said, as serious as a heart attack, "I like you."

"Th-thanks?" I tucked my hair behind my ear. "I mean, I guess you kind of have to since you're trying to make Rip jealous."

Banks's eyes flashed with something before he looked away and stood. "Yeah, well, if he doesn't make a move soon..."

"What? You'll drive him even more crazy?" I laughed.

He joined in. "Something like that. Now get to work. By the way, I checked out the blog last night along with your TikTok...three million followers and ten million views, not too shabby, Colby, not too shabby."

My cheeks heated at the compliment. "Thank you."

"My pleasure." He shot me a potentially devastating grin.

Something about the way he said "pleasure" had me feeling like I needed to take a cold shower, and he must have known because when he looked over his shoulder he winked, all before leaving me alone in Rip's office wondering what in the world had just happened.

Banks was a born flirt.

But was he actually flirting with me? And more importantly, did I want him to be?

Rip

"Uncle Rip, I hungry." Viera tugged at my shirt, looking up at me with adoration in her sparkly blue eyes. "Did you bring snacks?"

She was always hungry.

Always.

But the problem with Viera was that when she was hungry she was mean—as in make-a-grown-adult-cry-real-tears mean. So I'd learned to prepare for every possible scenario.

I reached into the diaper bag right when the jujitsu match was starting. Ben was down on the floor looking nervous as hell in his gi. He was going to be grappling with a kid who was a few inches taller, and even though Ben was really good, the kid had at least ten pounds on him.

With a sigh, I pulled out three different brands of

fruit snacks, a protein bar, a Zbar, Cheerios, and my secret weapon—Takis.

Monica had loved Takis, and Viera had wanted to be just like her mom, so when she was old enough to start snacking on different foods, she'd immediately taken to the Takis. Despite their spice, she was obsessed, but Monica had always been careful not to let Viera have too many since it wasn't necessarily a healthy snack.

"Takis!" Viera clapped her hands, then held them out. "Gimme!"

I held them out and moved my hand back and forth—her eyes followed left, right, then back to left again.

"Ah, hypnotism by way of Takis," came Colby's voice. "Smart man."

Before she even sat, she snatched them out of my hands, dug into the bag, and pulled a few out, then handed them to Viera and popped one in her own mouth.

"You like Takis too?" I asked, a bit surprised, like I was a monster who didn't understand junk food.

"Who do you think introduced Monica to them?" Colby grinned. "Let me guess, they're too messy for you, too spicy..."

She licked her fingers, and for some reason it didn't make me want to scowl or hurl.

It made me want to lick her fingers too.

And then lick something else.

What the *hell*? Had I accidentally hypnotized *myself* with the bag of Takis?

I gave my head a shake. "I don't mind them."

"Prove it." She held out the bag.

With a sigh I dug in and crunched down on a chip. Colby reached for my fingertips and looked like she wanted to lick off the remnants, then looked away toward where Ben stood on the mat.

"Look, Viera, Ben's about to go," she said, her eyes widening. "Whoa, that kid's huge."

"Yay, Ben!" Viera clapped. "Look, his turn!"

We watched as Ben did a little bow to his instructor and then to the kid he was fighting.

"Are we sure Ben's in the right weight class?" Colby's voice wobbled, and I knew she was thinking exactly what I was thinking. Ben was in trouble.

The kid immediately tried taking Ben down.

I flinched as Colby squeezed my thigh. "Go, Ben! Take him down! Flip him!"

"You know nothing about jujitsu, do you?"

"I tried googling on my way over to the bleachers and nearly got taken down by a ten-year-old with popcorn."

"Sounds about right." I nodded and then winced as Ben was thrown down. "That little shit!"

"Swear jar!" Viera sang.

"Swearing doesn't count in sports," Colby said.

"Go, little shit!" Viera yelled.

Colby slapped a hand over Viera's mouth as we earned several stares, then used her other hand to squeeze my thigh. "Let's go, Ben!"

I wasn't even sure if she knew she was doing it, but I suddenly didn't care as she squeezed harder and harder each time Ben was thrown down.

"What the hell is that kid's problem?" I lowered my voice so only Colby could hear me.

"I don't know, but I'd like to give him a flip!" She suddenly looked down at her hand and jerked it away. "Sorry."

"It's OK." Her cheeks were turning pink, and suddenly I found I couldn't look away.

She looked really pretty.

She also looked like she fit.

With us.

With everything.

With the chaos that was constantly banging around in my head. Ugh, I needed to sleep, right? That was what this was.

Her hair was half falling out of her bun, and her shirt could have used a good ironing, but suddenly all I saw was the kindness and caring and, yeah, embarrassment that shone on her face over the situation. The best part about Colby wasn't the perfection, no, it was the small imperfections she didn't care about that made her a good aunt.

So what if her shirt had a stain? She was busy coloring.

And her crazy hair? Well, there was glue up in there...put there by Ben the scientist.

I hated that things like that had set me off, because why the hell did they matter?

If the kids were happy.

If they were smiling.

If I was smiling...

And then Viera suddenly screamed again. "Bennnnn!"

Moment broken, all three of us stared while Ben suddenly did a double-leg takedown and pinned the little shit to the mat.

The kid's legs flailed beneath Ben, but he couldn't break the hold. You could see the strain on Ben's little face as he held strong.

Pride burst through my chest as Colby stood and yelled, "Get him, Ben!"

She didn't care that she had red-stained fingers from the Takis, or that she was yelling in front of all the parents.

No, she just cared about Ben.

That was it.

Maybe that had always been it.

Colby didn't seem to care what others thought. She only cared that the people she loved knew she loved them.

And what did that say about me? Always focused on everything being just right. Was I missing something in my pursuit of perfection? Was I missing the *entire* point?

Suddenly Colby threw both arms into the air and let out an earsplitting whoop. I glanced back down at the match just in time to see the ref call it in Ben's favor.

Ben looked up at the stands, finding us immediately and giving us a thumbs-up.

I gave him a thumbs-up back while Colby screamed, "Yay, Ben! I knew you could take him!"

Ben beamed at us. The first genuine smile I'd seen on his face since his parents' death. I never knew a smile could make me feel so horrible, but it did. Because he deserved to smile like that all the time.

Colby sat back down and smacked me on the thigh. "I'm killing that kid."

"What? What happened?"

"You didn't see that? Ben went to go shake that kid's hand, and the kid gave him a shove!"

I was on my feet instantly. "Where is he?"

I sounded like Batman, my voice deep, my expression murderous.

Colby's eyebrows shot up. "I think I like this version of you best."

Rage clouded my vision as I zeroed in on the pint-size punk. Before I knew what I was doing, I was stomping down the bleachers and over to the cocky little shit.

He was talking with his friends, and they were all yukking it up and congratulating him on getting in the last move on Ben. Their coach looked on, a smug smile on his face.

I'd deal with the coach later, but first I tapped the little shit on the shoulder. The kid was barely past my waist, but when he turned and looked up he was all puffed-up bravado. "What?"

"First off, you don't say, 'What' to an adult, you show respect, second, if someone offers to shake your hand, you shake their damn hand!"

"Sir," the coach intervened. "You can't be out on the floor."

"One minute." I held up my hand. "We're talking."

"Sir." Another coach approached, and then Ben was at my side.

"Uncle Rip, you can't be on the floor during matches."

"Apologize," I said to the kid.

The kid sighed and looked at Ben. "Your dad's weird."

"He's not my dad," Ben said. "My dad's in heaven. But this is my Uncle Rip, and he likes math!"

Math? Really? Was math my strongest attribute?

"Oh." The kid frowned. "Sorry 'bout your dad."

"Thanks," Ben said.

"Sir, you're going to need to come with me." A guy in a security uniform approached from the right.

I held up my hands. "I'm leaving, I'm leaving."

"Yes, you are." He jerked his head toward the door. "You can wait outside."

"You're kicking me out?" I asked incredulously, and then I realized every single person in the gym was staring at me: kids, parents, teachers, and even Colby, but she was smiling and gave me a thumbs-up as if to say, *Good job.*

"Fine," I grumbled, and I made my way toward the door with Ben on my tail and Colby and Viera joining me from the bleachers.

Once we were all outside, Colby cleared her throat. "So...you know I'm never going to let you live it down, right? Getting kicked out of a kids' sporting event?"

I hung my head. "I'm aware."

"But," she said, putting a hand on my shoulder, "I'm proud of you for sticking up for Ben. You're a good uncle." She squeezed. "Now who wants ice cream?"

The kids cheered.

And for some reason, all I kept thinking about was the loss of her hand on my shoulder when she lifted it, and the compliment she'd just given me, and how it made me feel like I was on top of the world.

THIRTEEN

Colby

It was late by the time we got home after ice cream, and I still had to write a blog post before I went to bed.

"Upstairs, kids," Rip said as we walked into the dark kitchen. "Brush your teeth and put on your pajamas. We'll both be up in a little bit to put you to bed."

"Can we sleep in the big bed again?" Ben asked in a sweet little voice. "Please?"

We were seriously creating some bad habits.

"Please, please, please," Viera mimicked him. "It smells like Mommy and Daddy in that room."

My throat got thick with emotion as I watched the look of horror pass across Rip's face.

"Sure, but just one more time," he said in a subdued tone, and I was thankful he'd answered because there was no way I could speak.

I had a feeling that promise wasn't going to stick, but I didn't say anything. Both kids sprinted up the stairs in a flurry of movement and stomps.

"That was nice of you," I whispered into the darkness. Neither of us moved to turn on the lights.

He was still, staring at the stairway, when I came up behind him and touched his arm. "Rip?"

"I miss them." His voice was barely audible.

It was the first time he'd offered it up without prompting. Apparently he did have a heart in that perfect body of his.

"I know you do," I said softly, almost afraid to say more since he was finally opening up. "Would it help if we talked about it?"

"No," he said quickly. "I just need to work through it."

"By not talking about it?"

"I look at the door a lot...," he went on, hanging his head. "I still imagine them walking back through it. I go to bed and I dream about it, only to wake up and be stuck in the nightmare."

"Our lives aren't a nightmare, Rip," I whispered. "You have two amazing little kids who adore you, great friends, a wonderful job..."

"But *they're* gone," he said. "And no matter what I have—I don't have them, not anymore."

I swallowed past the thickness in my throat. "You'll always have me."

I'd turned to go up the stairs when he reached for my hand and pulled me back against him, pulling me into his embrace for a tight hug.

I was so shocked I didn't know what to do other than wrap my arms around him and hold him tight.

He smelled like spice and warmth, his arms strong, holding me steady.

He rested his chin on my head and sighed. "I'm not usually a hugger."

"We can change that," I said against his chest.

His laugh was low, sexy. "I still think you're a hot mess."

"And I still think you have a perpetual stick up your ass."

"Good to know."

"Yup."

Neither of us pulled away.

"Uncle Rip!" Viera yelled down the stairs. "You're making a baby!"

I've never been shoved away from another human being so fast in my entire life.

"What?" This time, the look of horror that passed across his face was comical.

142

Viera giggled. "Mama says that if you cuddle really hard, your love creates a baby!"

Rip visibly paled.

I gave him a little shove. "You know that's not actually true, Rip."

"And yet the panic feels so real." He shuddered.

"Hey!" I crossed my arms. "That's hurtful!"

"We have two kids. We do not need two more."

"What makes you think we'd have *two* more, not one?"

"Sheer luck, you'd probably have triplets." Another shudder tore through him.

At least he wasn't shuddering at the idea of "cuddling" me, just at the idea of raising five children.

I looked around the messy living room.

At the kitchen with the bowls piled high in the sink.

And the toys strewn around the floor next to a Lego minefield. I found myself shuddering too. "Good point."

"See?" He nodded at my concession. "Viera, get into bed, sweetheart. We'll be right up."

"Yay!" She skipped off while we followed her up the stairs and down the hall into the master bedroom.

Monica and Brooks's clothes still hung in the closet, but we'd managed to put their personal items away in an effort to help the kids move on, as painful as that was. But it didn't matter that Monica's hairbrush was gone, or Brooks's favorite watch—it still felt like they were there, and I knew one day soon I'd have to go into that closet and put the last remaining pieces of their memory away.

Sometimes it felt like their ghosts existed in that room watching over the kids—over us. It wasn't creepy or even alarming that every time I stepped in that room I felt warm.

I felt their love.

I basked in it as I stood there and watched the kids tumble into the massive bed—Rip tickling Viera, Ben laughing at the scene.

I wondered how many times Monica and Brooks had done this at night. How many mornings had they woken up with those kiddos laughing and jumping on their bed and wished for just a few more minutes of sleep?

One thing I had already learned was that you had to hold on to the moments—even the ones that drove you crazy. Because you never knew how long you had to enjoy them.

"Aunt Colby!" Viera jumped to her feet on the bed. "Come tell us a story!"

"Ooooh, a story?" I echoed, forcing a sense of

lightness into my voice with great effort. "Hmmm, what kind of story do you want?"

"A funny one!" she sang, and then she plopped onto her butt. "But you have to lay in the middle with Uncle Rip, it's rules."

"Oh, well, if it's rules." I shared a smile with him and crawled toward the middle of the bed with Viera on my left, Rip on my right, and Ben with his head on Rip's shoulder.

Anyone seeing this scene would think we were the perfect family.

Looks can be so deceiving, can't they?

I racked my brain trying to think of a good story and laughed when, for some reason, I thought of my horrible first—and last—date with Rip.

"So there was once this servant girl who was in love with the prince," I started, and I laughed when Ben groaned. "Hey, we'll tell a bloody story next!"

"OK!" he said quickly, and he went quiet again.

"Anyway..." I cleared my throat. "She was really loud where the prince was quiet, she was messy, he was clean, she almost always had some sort of stain on her shirt." I could feel Rip stiffen beside me, but I didn't dare look his way. "But one day the handsome prince decided to take her on a picnic. She was so nervous that she spilled pop on herself and on him, and when he leaned in to help her, she thought he was going to give her true love's kiss!"

Viera sighed. "They were going to make a baby!"

I nearly choked but recovered quickly. "Well, I'm not sure about that," I said before continuing. "He didn't kiss her. He was just trying to clean up the pop, so she got super embarrassed and ran away..." Why the hell would I tell this story again?

Viera sighed. "Did he chase her?"

"No," Rip finished. "But he should have. That's what a good prince does...right, Viera?"

Really? Was that what he really thought? I turned my head to find Rip staring right at me, his eyes flashing as he slid his hand across the bed and squeezed mine. "You always chase the girl, even if she drives you crazy. A true gentleman always apologizes. He doesn't make girls cry."

"I don't make girls cry," Ben piped up.

I couldn't speak as Rip held my hand tight.

I didn't trust my voice.

And a stupid tear slid down my cheek.

Rip saw it.

He released my hand quickly and spoke. "He didn't go after her, but if he had, he would have said, 'Let's go on a picnic again, and I'm sorry I made you sad.'

Princes sometimes don't have the best manners, and what Aunt Colby didn't share is that this prince lost his parents just like you guys."

I tried not to flinch when he mentioned a story I already knew—his story, their story, the one that set Monica and Rip on a path so vastly different from everyone else's.

One that Monica told me the day we became best friends.

It was easier not thinking about it, because it made Monica sad and it made Rip go into protective mode. The fact that he was even talking about it shocked me.

He continued with his story, and I tried to keep the tears in. He was opening up, and it broke me to hear his voice say these words, tell this story. "He was sad and angry, and he took it out on the servant girl because she was kind. Sometimes when we feel things on the inside that we don't understand, we get angry on the outside."

"Like you got angry today at jujitsu?" Ben asked innocently.

I covered my mouth so the kids wouldn't see my smile.

"Yes." He shot me a smirk. "Like today at jujitsu."

"Cool." Ben yawned. "That was gangster, Uncle Rip."

I mouthed, "What the heck?" to Rip.

"Yup." Rip nodded. "Straight gangster, yo…"

My eyes flew open wide and a laugh slipped out. "Never say that again."

"Uncle Rip's so ollllld." Ben joined in my laughter, and then Viera was laughing, and we were a group of giggling adults and kids.

It felt nice.

I wanted to exist in that moment forever.

But too soon it was gone.

And the kids were sleepy.

We said our good nights, kissing each of them on the forehead, then closed the door and silently walked back downstairs.

Exhausted, I went into the kitchen to tackle the dishes since I knew dirty dishes piling up were one of Rip's many pet peeves.

He came up behind me, his breath on my neck. My entire body tensed, then relaxed into him as I leaned back, willing him to kiss down my neck. He hesitated and I counted one breath, two. And then, "Go relax, I'll do the dishes."

"No, it's fine, I can just—"

"Just because you think of yourself like a servant girl doesn't mean you are one. Go sit. You still have to post your content, right?"

A shiver ran down my spine, a shiver of excitement. "You remembered?" I still hadn't turned around.

"You'd be surprised what I remember," was his cryptic reply. "Grab your computer and sit on the couch so you can get comfortable and into the zone."

"OK." I kind of liked being bossed around by him, not that I'd ever admit it out loud.

I walked away and didn't look back. I didn't have to, I knew his shirtsleeves would be shoved up past amazing tan forearms, and I knew he'd look hotter than anyone had a right to while doing dishes.

Ugh. I had to stop. I wasn't a servant-turned-princess like Cinderella, and Rip was no prince.

I grabbed my laptop and sat on the couch, immersed in my work until I started getting sleepy. The next thing I knew, I was getting tapped on the shoulder. I jolted awake and groaned as I felt drool running down my chin. "Whyyyy...?"

"Was that a general question, or are you asking why I'm saving you from sleeping like a human pretzel?"

"Too many words." I yawned. "What time is it?"

"Ten." He offered an apologetic smile.

"Oh no!" I scrambled for my laptop and quickly opened it, my brain still fuzzy from falling asleep on the couch. Phew, at least I'd finished the hard part before I'd face-planted onto the couch.

While I waited for my post to load so I could grab my next assignment, I felt him looking over my shoulder. "You trying to be creepy and invasive, or is it just a Friday?"

"You have over three million followers." He sounded stunned, like it was a big deal. Did he not understand the power of social media? Instagram? TikTok? If people had that many followers, they not only had to continue to put out content, but they had to do it weekly, otherwise they lost followers or viewership, which meant lost money. How did he not get that?

"Yup, and my goal is to get two million more."

"That's a lot."

Why did he sound so surprised? "Did you think I was only writing these for my health? Or my grandma?"

His eyebrows lifted up a bit. "But...all those people follow...you?"

"Yes, I know." I sniffed and rubbed my eyes. "But regardless of your opinion, I'm not always a hot mess." Probably a bad time to continue to wipe the drool from my chin, but whatever.

Rip crossed his arms. "Oh, really?"

"Really." I lifted my chin in defiance. "People even

want to have sex with me. Male people, not just like boyfriends, not that I have a boyfriend—that's not the point!"

He coughed out a laugh. "No, keep going. I want to hear about all these . . . people."

"I hate you."

"Feeling's mutual." He sat next to me and smiled.

"Ugh, and here I thought we'd waved the white flag."

"Maybe I just like provoking you."

"Feeling's mutual," I echoed.

"Touché." He laughed. "So what's this post about? More food?"

"Don't hate on the food. Food is life," I said with a triumphant smile. "This is about food in Scotland. I was supposed to go before . . ." My voice trailed off, but I forced myself to recover. "Before everything."

He nodded. "But you had to cancel, right?"

"Yeah." I shrugged. "It was a research trip. I was really excited about it."

"I'm surprised it wasn't some tropical destination," he joked with a smile.

I frowned. "Huh? Why?"

And now it was time for him to look away. "I may have assumed that you stay at nice hotels, eat their food, then post about it and get kickbacks. I didn't know there was actual research. Is this the part where I tell you I'm a jackass and I'm sorry?"

"Yup. Read the room, Rip, read the room."

"I'm sorry."

"It's OK." I checked out the freshly posted content. "I know the digital world is hard for dinosaurs like yourself to understand."

"I deserved that."

"Yup."

Without any warning he got up and left. So still a jackass...noted. I heard some rummaging in the kitchen and had dived back into my work when suddenly a glass appeared in front of my laptop.

"What's this?"

"Whisky. Neat." The glass was clear, one ice cube and at least two inches of whisky were in it, and the man handing it to me? With his dark hair, gorgeous eyes, and wicked smile, yeah, he wasn't bad either.

"And you're handing me this for what? Some sort of weird manly peace offering where I get drunk and talk about stocks and bonds or..."

"It's the best I could do." He sat down next to me on the couch. "But Edinburgh by far is the best location for a whisky tasting, in my opinion. It could be the castle nearby, the way that the Highlands call out to you, or even the Witchery by the Castle, an eatery just down the street that feels like it's built inside a cave. It's one of those places that you just know someone had to have gotten murdered in back in the day." He laughs. "It's Gothic, beautiful, and exactly what you should write about. I think that's my top favorite—" He stopped talking and tapped my screen. "Shouldn't you be taking notes?"

I choked down the whisky and rasped, "I can't decide if I hate you more, or if I should say thank you. It's very confusing and quite frankly alarming. Um... should I feel hot?"

He smirked. "It's the whisky."

Was it, though? "Right, right, so whisky, castle." I set the glass down and started adding to my post. "And cave murder. Nice."

"Type in 'the Witchery,'" he said.

I quickly pulled up the website and sighed. "One day."

"One day," he echoed. "When life isn't..." He glanced at the still-dirty kitchen. Well, at least the dishes were done. "This."

I let out a snort. "Please, that's normal for me."

Rip's eyes widened in horror.

"Gotcha." I winked. "That's Satan's pigsty, and I have a feeling it's gonna be like that until we figure out how to balance our new...life."

"We'll get there."

"Yeah," I agreed. "We will."

We stared at one another for a few seconds before he cleared his throat and looked away. It was the first time his green eyes had lingered on mine that something unspoken had passed between us.

All this time I used to think it was annoyance.

Now I knew.

There was something there, wasn't there?

I hadn't been wrong two years before.

I frowned.

He looked into his drink.

"Hey, Rip," I said.

"Yeah." He was still staring down into the amber liquid.

"Do you hate me?"

He didn't flinch. Didn't smile. Just stared into his drink and whispered, "I wish I could."

Not what I was expecting, so I forced a laugh. "Compliment or insult?"

His eyes met mine briefly as he threw back his drink and whispered, "Guess."

Uncomfortable, I looked away. "It's the grief, though, right?"

He was silent for a minute, then said, "It's life, Colby. It's fucking life."

FOURTEEN

Rip

I'd been dreading this moment for the past two and a half weeks. The day we officially boxed up all Monica and Brooks's clothes. Ben was at his friend James's house, and Viera was next door with Mrs. Harris making cookies. It just made sense to have them out of the house.

It was going to be hard enough on *us*, let alone them.

My chest tightened as I stood outside the master bedroom, unable to walk past the door even though Colby was already in the closet boxing their clothes away.

Why was watching her fold a shirt into a donation box just as hard as watching the caskets being lowered into the cold, hard ground?

I braced my hands against the doorframe and took a deep breath, then took one step, then another, until I was right outside the large closet watching Colby gently take clothes off hangers and fold them into the large boxes for Goodwill.

I wondered if she realized her hands were shaking.

Did she notice the tears streaming down her face?

Or was she choosing to be numb like me? It was the only way I could get through this without cracking.

"Hey..." My voice caught in my throat.

Her eyes flickered toward mine and then back to the shirt in her hands. There was nothing special about it except it had a glitter butterfly on it. It had been Monica's favorite, hell, butterflies had been an obsession for Monica since we were kids. All it took was one trip to the local zoo when they had the butterfly exhibit and she was convinced that she actually was one. Years later she said that once she died, she'd come back as a beautiful butterfly.

"Don't talk about dying." I gave her a light shove and ran toward the swing set.

She stuck out her tongue. "Everyone dies, dum-dum! Why not choose how awesome you can be when you come back? I read about it in a book once."

"You're twelve," I pointed out.

"And you're a gross boy." She sat on the swing. "Now push me super high like the butterfly I'll be in the sky."

I smiled to myself. "Like the butterfly in the sky."

She gripped the swing and closed her eyes. "You'll see. Maybe one day you'll be lucky enough to see a butterfly like me."

I rolled my eyes. "Sure, OK."

"I think I'd be blue."

"Why blue?"

"Duh, it's the color of the sky." She laughed. "What would you come back as? If you could choose? Dirt?"

"Hilarious." I smiled despite her insult. "If you get to come back as a butterfly, so do I. After all, we gotta stick together, but at least make my color cool."

"You can be yellow."

"Fair." I pushed her higher. "You be blue, I'll be yellow."

"Deal." She laughed. "Now push me higher!"

My heart caught in my throat.

Why?

Just why?

I looked down at it as she tossed it into a box.

"Ben made that for her last year during parents' week."

As if this couldn't get worse. I sucked in the stupid tears. "Maybe we should keep it, then? Since he made it?" I offered.

"I'm stuck," she said suddenly as she grabbed another shirt. "Between wanting to burn everything that makes us remember them and wanting to hoard it all so we don't forget." At a loss for words, I just stood there.

She shrugged, then sat on the floor next to the box. "I have nothing that will help or make this better, all I have is..." Her voice caught. "All I have is me, which I know isn't enough, but I have me, Rip. So if you need to let it go, if that's what you need right now—" She met my gaze. "I'm here. I can be your mess. I can be the chaos you need."

I dropped more clothes into the box and then sighed. "I used to believe in God, and then..." I grabbed another shirt and folded it. "It was too soon, Colby. And it wasn't fair."

"I know," she whispered, her eyes filling with tears. "Nothing about this has been fair."

"No." I looked away so she wouldn't see the emotion on my face. "You think that they feel us? That they hear us?"

Damn it.

I'd been so horrible to her, and now I was asking her for comfort.

"Are you asking because you don't believe in magic or fairy tales, or are you asking because you need to?"

she asked gently, in that same voice that made me want to both pull her close and push her away.

The shirt dropped from my hands and fell in a flutter against the floor as I hung my head. "I think sometimes, even adults need a bit of a fairy tale."

"Then." She walked up next to me, so close I could smell her flowery perfume. She grabbed my hand firmly in hers, not gently, but in a way that said, *I'm here, I'm always here.* "I think that Brooks probably knows you're in his closet stealing his clothes and being emotional. I think Monica is both crying and laughing over our antics with their kids. But most of all, I think that they're looking at us, smiling and saying...*Good job. Survival of the fittest.*" She grinned. "Because that was them."

"That was them," I repeated with a small smile, wishing we could stay in this moment forever. I had no idea what it meant, but it was something, and something was better than whatever the hell I'd been trying to navigate for weeks.

I would take something with Colby over nothing any day.

And that's when it hit me.

Colby.

She made me want to jump off the nearest roof

while at the same time I was scared that if I got too close, I'd want her to stay with me, like this, forever.

What a fucking terrifying feeling that was.

"Yes," I said again. "It was definitely them."

And now it was just us.

Me and her.

Her and me.

Us.

She stared at a shirt with "Mama" in pink glitter across the front. "Do you think Viera would want to maybe keep this?"

I opened my mouth, then shut it and shook my head. It was all I was capable of doing as I took the shirt from her hands and put it into the box between us. Colby had said she would try to get most of Monica's stuff out of there so I didn't have to deal with it—which meant I needed to start on Brooks's side of the closet. The mood was morose, heavy, as I started going through his suits.

They were expensive.

And in pristine condition.

I knew that he'd be happy that they would one day help someone maybe get a job or give someone confidence.

With each suit I pulled off the hanger, I would get

a whiff of his cologne, and then I would get hammered with memory after memory.

College.

Our trip to Thailand.

His wedding day.

I didn't realize I'd stopped folding until Colby put a hand on my shoulder. "Why don't I just finish all of this up."

Not wanting to be the weak link, I shook my head no and kept on working in silence.

Once the closet was nearly empty, I moved over to the row of shelves in the back and grabbed another box sitting next to the linens. It broke open as soon as I pulled it forward, spilling the contents onto the floor in one big bright and traumatic heap.

"What the hell?" A buzzing sounded from beneath the pile, and then I looked back at the broken box.

In giant red letters it said "Burn Box."

"What's that noise?" Colby walked over, and immediately her cheeks turned bright red. "Oh my gosh. I totally forgot about this!"

"What is that sound—"

I picked up the towel that had fallen on top of the items making noise and recoiled so fast I knocked the rest of the towels off the shelf.

Colby burst out laughing as I stumbled backward and fell onto my ass. "Are those *sex toys*?" I asked.

"What else is shaped like a—"

"Don't finish that sentence!" I pointed an accusing finger at her. "Make it go away!"

She just laughed harder, more tears running down her face. "Monica and Brooks liked it dirty!"

I was seriously going to cut off my own ears.

"Please, Colby. I'm begging you. Make them disappear. I will never unsee this!"

Colby reached into the pile.

"That's not even close to being sanitary!" I swatted her hand away. "Don't touch anything, oh shit, I think I'm going to puke."

Colby fell back onto the floor laughing. "This is my favorite moment ever!"

"It's not funny!" I said, momentarily horrified.

"Oh, it's hilarious."

"At least turn off the vibrator!"

Her grin took on a wicked quality. "Nah, I think it adds to the current mood, right?"

I glared, and she switched it off with a sigh and a red face.

"Why the hell would they need this many sex toys? There's at least seven different types of...devices."

Colby grinned. "Huh. I never knew you were such a prude."

"I'm not! It's just, it's my sister! And nobody wants to think about those...things." I cleared my throat. "You know, with their sister, and can we stop talking about this now? I'm already going to have nightmares for life."

As if ignoring me, Colby kept talking. "It's funny, we always had these ridiculous conversations where we went over what to burn or what to take care of if anything happened to us." Tears filled her eyes. "But this? I never imagined this." She swiped her cheeks. "She was good, you know? Hilarious. Just such a good person."

I put a hand on Colby's shoulder and said, "She was the best."

"The very best."

"She also chose the best."

"What?" Colby looked up at me, bright-blue eyes shining with tears. "What do you mean?"

"Only that she was a great judge of character, and although"—I leaned down and cupped her chin—"I'm still horrified that you're half an adult...you've been like a sister to her."

"And to you too?" Colby asked.

I felt like I'd swallowed something too large, my heart felt too big in my chest, and the room felt too small. "Yeah, me too."

Lame.

Colby deflated instantly, and I wanted to punch myself.

I'd had one perfect moment to tell her that I was attracted to her, to tell her that amid her chaos and constant need to talk she pulled me, and instead I was pretty sure I'd just called her my fucking sister.

Damn it!

Colby pulled away and changed the subject. "She told me that if anything ever happened to her to burn the box in the closet. At the time I thought she was being dramatic." Colby picked up what looked like a spreader bar with cuffs attached to it. "Huh, same one from *Fifty Shades*, nice."

I rubbed my eyes, hoping to get the vision of Monica and the spreader bar out of my mind. It didn't work, probably because Colby was still holding it up as if fascinated by the locking mechanisms. "How does this even attach?" And wouldn't Monica with all her matchmaking ways have just loved that?

I almost laughed.

Instead I watched as Colby threw the contraption

around, still unable to figure it out until I said, "Wrists to ankles." Whoops.

Her eyes lit up with interest. "And how would you know?"

"It's obvious," I lied as my cheeks heated. It's not like I had one, but I wasn't dumb and I'd been curious back when the movie came out, sue me. "I mean, I am a guy. I know the mechanics of...handcuffs. Wow, this is just getting worse, isn't it?"

"Yes, I think you should keep talking." Colby nodded. "But it's fascinating. Tell me more about mechanics, Rip."

I shot her a glare. "We can't donate this. Nobody at the Goodwill wants secondhand sex toys."

"Can you imagine? Dear old Grandpa walking in and looking for some sturdy handcuffs..." She started to laugh and then wiped a tear from her eyes. "Monica would haunt us for life."

"Probably." I wrapped an arm around her. "But at least they left us something to laugh about...there's been too many tears."

"So many." She sniffled. "Sorry for being a wreck."

I wanted to say sorry for staying too strong, for not crying, for not showing that I was mourning too. Instead I just held Colby close. "You're not a wreck."

"Yeah." She sighed. "I am."

"Then you're a perfect mess...a perfect wreck...let yourself be the masterpiece of chaos."

"Won't that piss you off?"

"Me?" I hugged her tighter. "Nah, I think I'm beginning to think that the truly beautiful things in this world aren't perfect. I don't want perfect."

"Y-you don't?"

"No," I said honestly. "I don't."

"Anyway," she sighed. "Should we just keep it or bury it? The last thing we need is anyone finding it and thinking it's, you know..."

My brain went in all the wrong directions.

"Let's just keep the box for now," I said when I'd found my voice.

"Wait, to use for later?" Her cheeks pinked. "I mean, not us, no, not that, I mean, like, why would we keep them?"

I pinched her arm. "I'm not into strawberry-flavored lube, I prefer chocolate." Where the hell had that come from? "Let's keep them so that whenever we get too sad we can come in here and laugh. I'm tired of being sad, aren't you?"

"Yeah." She smiled. "I really am."

"Good. It's done, then."

"Sooooo, chocolate?" she asked.

"Not another word."

"But you said—"

"—Colby."

She pulled away. "Thank you, by the way, for being so strong. I cry over a T-shirt and you're ready to box things away..."

"Honestly," I said, looking away, teeth clenched. "If I start, I won't stop, Colby. That's not strength, that's more like weakness and avoidance."

"We all deal with grief differently," she whispered after a few seconds.

"Yeah." I stared at the pile of sex toys, then very carefully started putting them into a new box. A few Polaroids fell out of the last remnants of the pile and it was like a bomb going off in that closet.

They all fell facedown.

I stared at them.

Colby stared at them.

"I'm both curious and horrified," she whispered.

"There's no coming back from this," I agreed, reaching for them. "You look, I don't want to see my sister naked."

"Well, I don't want to see my two best friends naked! I walked in on them once in college and I'm still traumatized!"

"He was so loud, how did you not know what they were doing?"

"How do you know that?"

"Roommates." I winced. "Trust me, I wish I didn't know what he sounded like when he orgasmed."

She nudged me. "OK, help me put this on the top shelf so the kids don't find it."

"That's just what we need. Ben grabbing a vibrator and then bringing his new toy to show-and-tell."

Colby shuddered. "I'd just tell the school that you're into some really strange kink."

I laughed. "Oh, is that so?"

"Yeah, I don't want to go to the principal's office. I've never been."

I gawked. "You've never been to the principal's office?"

"I hate, and I do mean *hate*, getting into trouble."

I wondered if that made it harder coexisting with me in a space where I was always correcting her.

"Makes sense," I finally said as Colby got up on the small stepladder she'd been using and tried to put the box on the top shelf.

Her foot slipped, and she wobbled back and forth trying to catch herself, but suddenly she was falling backward.

She slammed against my chest so hard, the breath left my lungs. I scrambled to catch her and fell to the floor with her on top of me.

"Ouch." She winced. "Sorry."

I didn't realize how close she really was until I could see the specks of sparkling green in her bright-blue eyes.

"You have really pretty eyes," I blurted like an idiot.

Mine chose that exact moment to flicker to her mouth, and my heart started pounding so hard in my chest I knew she could feel it.

She lowered her head while I lifted mine.

And just when I was about to touch my lips to hers...

The doorbell rang.

FIFTEEN

Colby

"You're like a bad cold." I sighed and opened the door wider to let Banks in. He was wearing perfectly tight, black ripped jeans that were molded to his body and a graphic T-shirt that had some sort of band's name scribbled over it.

"I think that was a compliment," he said. "You ready to go?" He stepped inside and looked around the house. "It's cleaner than last time. Has Rip learned his lesson yet, or did he hire maids?"

"Why are you here?" Rip grumbled as he stomped down the stairs.

"Did we break up?" Banks looked around the room. "I'm your friend. Friends often stop by other friends' houses, especially when taking friends to the movies."

I frowned. "You guys are going to the movies?"

"No, we are." Banks wrapped an arm around me. "So, like I said, are you ready?"

"Hold up a second." Rip held out his hands. "We had plans today."

"Plans?" Banks frowned. "Like what?"

I wanted to say, "Yeah, like what?" since we'd already finished the closet; instead I just watched Rip sweat.

"We were cleaning out the closets..." Rip cleared his throat and shared a look with me that said, *Don't say a word.*

"But we finished just a few minutes ago," I pointed out. "And the kids are going to be out until dinner."

Rip suddenly smiled. "You're right, I'll just go get my jacket."

My jaw dropped. "You hate the movies."

"No, I hate romantic comedies, I don't hate all movies."

"This is a romantic comedy." Banks seemed to be enjoying himself as he looked between us. "But if you think you can stomach it—"

"I'll be fine," Rip blurted, and then he eyed me up and down. "Why don't you change into—"

"Finish that sentence, see what happens." I parked my hands on my hips and offered him my fiercest glare because here's the thing, I was fully aware that I wasn't wearing a pantsuit like Heather. I owned zero designer earrings or shoes with red bottoms and yes, maybe I was feeling insecure about it, but the point was, he'd almost kissed me. What had happened to him not wanting perfect?

Whatever, we both got caught up in the moment. Nothing more. And the fact was, I wouldn't change my chaos for perfection any day, even if it gave me the sweats along with chest pain, because.

Life.

These kids represented life.

A life that might be messy, and sad, but it was joyful too.

So if I was the one who made Rip shake his head at the chaos of it all, well, good on me.

Good. On. Me.

Rip scowled and held up his hands in innocence. "I was just saying..."

"Good call on not finishing that sentence. Plus she always looks beautiful, even in head-to-toe black sweats and a..." He pointed at my head. "Is that a bun or a ponytail?"

I groaned. "Maybe I should change."

Rip let out a snort.

"I'm sorry, did you want to say something?" I crossed my arms.

His face paled. "Nothing at all."

"Be right back, Banks." I smiled and then shot Rip another glare and stomped up the stairs with him following closely behind. My hands shook as I tried to process the fact that just minutes ago we'd almost kissed. Was Rip possessed? Drunk? Did he actually want to kiss me, or had it been brought on by exhaustion? I was ready to strangle Banks because we'd probably never have a moment like that again and all I wanted was to rip it apart, tear it to pieces, dissect it and put it back together like a puzzle.

The kiss.

The almost-kiss that had never happened but could have. Rip and I didn't say anything to each other, and when we reached the top of the stairs, where the almost-kiss had happened, he went left and I went right. Five minutes later I was coming back down the same hallway wearing jeans and a T-shirt along with combat boots, and he approached from the opposite direction, somehow looking even better than Banks in a similar T-shirt and jeans.

"After you." He held out his hand toward the stairs, his throat moving in a slow swallow as he eyed my mouth for two seconds before clearing his throat and looking away.

I defaulted to teasing because I wasn't sure how to handle something of this magnitude.

"Be honest, you just don't want me to trip you on the way down," I teased.

"Figured that was an actual possibility." His smile was back, but this time it was softer, different. The temptation to open my big mouth and demand he give me answers was strong, almost as strong as every homicidal tendency I'd had since moving in with him.

"You know you don't have to come," I said quickly to gauge his reaction. At this point I'd take a slight flinch on his part, an eyebrow raise, any sort of hesitation or clue that I wasn't having a mental breakdown earlier while he was simply trying to grab an eyelash from my cheek or whisper hateful things across my lips. "Especially if you're going to sit there being grumpy the entire time."

He rolled his eyes, and just like that we were back in default mode, kiss ignored. "Me, grumpy?"

"You're kidding, right?"

We reached the bottom of the stairs. The air felt tense between us, heavy even. Banks was rummaging through the semiempty fridge. "Do you guys really not have soda in here? Beer?"

"Get out of there." Rip sighed, then cleared his throat like he was uncomfortable. Or regretting our near-kiss. Probably that. Definitely that. "We're ready."

"Good. I was really looking forward to being the third wheel today." Banks pulled his head out of the fridge and shut it. "You look beautiful."

"Thanks," Rip answered before I could. "I'll drive."

The drive turned out to be twenty minutes of tension during which Banks complimented me every few minutes while Rip swerved as if dodging squirrels and trying out for NASCAR.

Once in the theater, before I could even sit down, Rip took the seat on my left and Banks settled in on my right. The movie was two hours of romantic comedy about two men fighting over one woman.

And there I sat.

Wondering.

Wishing.

Battling my own feelings over the fact that I was getting the very strong sense that Banks actually liked me, and yet the guy I couldn't stop pining over was on my other side wearing a perpetual frown.

Why?

Why did it have to be Rip, out of all people in this universe?

It was equal parts wanting to launch myself at him and wanting to strangle him and I hated it. I'd always wondered if it was because he didn't feel the same way, but emotional overload or not, he'd almost kissed me in that closet.

And not just that, he did things, small things that I noticed that nobody else seemed to. With all his grumpy tendencies, he always opened doors for people. He tipped double what he should even when buying his boring-ass coffee, and he loved the kids—truly loved them, didn't just pretend to love them, then take them to Target so they told everyone how awesome he was for buying them toys.

He spent time.

That was what got me.

Time had always been my love language, the one thing that spoke to me on a spiritual level, so while I wanted to chase him around the kitchen, the fact that he put down his phone when the kids were talking to him—when anyone was talking to him—or that he read with them every night or sat down for dinner and was actually present, asking everyone, myself included, what they'd done that day?

It was a dream.

A miracle, really.

He cared. He actually cared. And after a lifetime of

disastrous dates where guys would be on Tinder while sitting across from me during dinner or, worse, asking about my ten-year plan—he never did that. Sure he made fun of my job, and he drove me crazy, but when he was talking to me, he was present. He really listened.

And sure, Rip was also a jackass.

A pain *in* my ass.

But he was a rare male—one whom I stupidly compared every guy to.

Banks included.

As if on cue, Banks's elbow nudged mine before he turned and winked at me. The guy was way too good looking, it wasn't fair, and I wished in that moment I could like someone like Banks.

Instead it was grumpy butt on my left currently holding all available space in my heart.

Damn it.

Would this movie ever end?

I exhaled a sigh of relief when the credits finally rolled and the lights turned on, only to stumble against Banks as I stood up.

Rip rolled his eyes and muttered, "Get a room."

"Your encouragement is noted." Banks winked.

I sighed. "I tripped on my shoelace."

"Surprise, surprise," Rip said in a dry tone. "Your shoes aren't tied."

"I'll tie them—" Banks lowered himself to the ground while Rip ground his teeth in annoyance. That my shoes were untied? That someone else was tying them? Or that he was thinking about the tension between us too, confused, and hating it?

Ha, nice fairytale thought there, Colby.

I shook my head as Banks stood. "All done!"

Rip stared him down, his expression unreadable, the air thick with tension even though neither guy was really saying anything.

"Is there a reason you invited yourself?" I asked sweetly. "I thought you didn't like rom-coms?"

"Is there a reason you can't stop gawking at Banks every time he opens his damn mouth?" he said right back, making me pause. Was he...jealous? Banks had barely touched me all night—he'd tied my shoes, for crying out loud—it wasn't like he'd proposed marriage with one knee pressed against the sticky floor of the movie theater.

"What's wrong with you?" I clenched my fists. "I thought things..." I didn't finish the sentence because I didn't want to look stupid or sound stupid. What I wanted to say was that I'd thought things had shifted, that we'd gone from bickering and biting each other's heads off to actually attempting to get along, not just for the kids but for us. Had this whole Banks intervention ruined everything?

"So." Banks rubbed his hands together. "I think I'm just going to take an Uber back." Banks actually looked pleased with himself, as if he'd accomplished something between us, when his idea had completely backfired.

At least earlier this week I hadn't been fighting with Rip.

Now we were back to square one.

"Don't be dramatic," Rip said to Banks. "Your car's at our house anyway."

"No, no, it's fine, really." His smile was so arrogant I had a sudden urge to trip him. "Oh, and I was thinking maybe dinner next week? We can try that new sushi place."

Rip tensed next to me for the millionth time that night.

"Oh, um . . . maybe." I gulped, not knowing what else to say but needing this whole awkward scenario to be done with before I passed out from the stress. "I'll have to see if it's OK with Rip, only because the kids—"

"Why would I care if you went on a date?" Rip said coolly. "Go, I'll watch the kids while you two go out. Sounds fun."

"Oh." I tried not to let him see the rejection on my face. I was getting whiplash from his responses. Why was it that this one hurt the worst? I'd rather have him angry at me or fighting with me than tell me to go on a date with his best friend as if it didn't bother him when it actually bothered me, like I was getting passed off to someone else because he couldn't be troubled. "All right, then—"

"Great." Banks interrupted almost like he wanted to get the yes before he bolted away from us at top speed. "I'll text."

He was gone in seconds, leaving me alone with a very irritated-looking Rip and a half-eaten bag of the popcorn that was already starting to sit heavily in my stomach.

Rip didn't say anything as we both walked out of the theater and toward his car. He at least opened the door for me, letting me go through first, then opened the passenger-side door to the car and shut it.

See? Manners even when he was irritated.

I ignored the pain in my chest as he walked around the car and got in.

I checked my phone to see if things were going OK with Mrs. Harris and saw a reminder to make Ben's cupcakes.

"Did you make Ben's cupcakes for tomorrow?"

"Shoot." Rip took a turn and pulled into the grocery store parking lot, then cut the engine and unbuckled his seat belt. "You find more stuff for the gluten-free, soy-free, fun-free cupcakes so they don't taste like shit, and I'll get milk."

"You forgot sugar-free," I added. "And dairy-free."

"What are we going to put in them? Air?" He seemed frustrated, but I knew it wasn't about the cupcakes.

"Hey, Rip." I fell into step with him. "If you don't want me to go on a date with Banks I won't. Honestly, he's just a friend anyway." I frowned. "And I could be totally off base, but you seem more prickly than usual, like a pet porcupine that just shed all of their quills."

"Yeah, he definitely doesn't see you as a friend, Colby. Also that would make me a naked porcupine, so thanks for that analogy."

I laughed and gave him a little shove. "You know what I meant."

Some of the tension left his shoulders as he stopped walking next to me and hung his head. "I don't know what sane man would see you as just a friend."

He cursed under his breath. "You're like a fucking hurricane—a chaotic beautiful mess of waves and wind, powerful, daunting, and any guy—especially ones like Banks—would risk his life during the storm just to see if he can survive it."

I sucked in a sharp breath. Had he just said what I thought he'd said? Goose bumps rose all over my body as I waited for him to say more. Instead he squeezed his eyes shut, and I knew stress had sent him over the edge, he'd meant to keep the words in his head but had blurted them out instead. His body language had gone from smooth, arrogant, confident, to suddenly panicked as he licked his lips, bit down, then shoved a hand in his pocket only to pull it out.

"I'm confused." I nudged him again. "Am I killing him, or is he just getting rained on?" I asked with a laugh.

Rip smirked and turned to me. "I wouldn't mind if you killed him."

I shoved him lightly. "Be mature."

"I'm always mature, that's probably the problem. See, Banks is the type of guy that goes into a grocery store and probably thinks, *You know what would be fun? A produce aisle race.* I'm the type of guy who goes into the grocery store and says, 'Oh, look, beef's on sale.'"

I burst out laughing. "Are you calling yourself boring?"

"I'm calling myself reliable. And maybe sometimes boring, too mature for my own good...Monica always—" He stopped himself, closed his eyes for a moment, then took a deep breath and opened them again. "Monica always knew what to do to get me out of my shell, and now it just feels like things are closing in even more." He sighed. "And shit, I did not mean to just dump all of my emotions onto you like that. I'm sorry, let's just get the food and go. I'm fine, everything's fine, it's been a long day and even longer night with one of my best friends watching you eat popcorn instead of the movie for two and a half painful hours."

"Was it really that awful?" I asked.

"If *awful* means there was a moment I nearly lost all sanity and control and smacked the popcorn out of your hands, then yeah, it was that awful."

"Are we having a moment here?" I teased. We were literally flirting in the middle of the produce section, and it felt more like a date than the movie had. "You know, where you're opening up and actually talking about your feelings...insecurities, that sort of thing?"

"Do not"—he pointed a finger at me—"get used to it."

His eyes flickered to my mouth again before he jerked his head away. "We should probably"—he gulped— "find...things."

Insecure Rip might be my new favorite. He'd started walking away when I grabbed him by the arm.

"Wait!" He stopped, and I jerked my hand away. "You know, now that you mention it...a little race might be fun. But you know what would be more fun?" I was either going to crash and burn or this would be another moment when I could get him out of his shell— the way Monica used to.

I could have sworn I heard her laugh, felt her warm smile, and wondered if there wasn't one more reason they'd decided to leave the kids to both of us.

One very important reason.

"Oh God." Rip looked heavenward. "I gave you ideas, didn't I?"

"Answer the question." I grinned triumphantly.

"What?" He shoved his hands into his pockets like he was bored, but the corners of his lips twitched with a slight smile. "What would be more fun?"

"A game."

"What kind of game?" He sounded about as enthusiastic as someone going in for a root canal.

"One where you have to find three of the most

awkward items they sell at a grocery store—and put them in the cart."

"Wait, so we have to actually purchase said items?" he asked, his eyes slightly widening.

"Yup!"

"Are we in high school?" He rolled his eyes.

"Hey, you're the one who said Monica got you out of your shell—there was a reason I was her best friend."

"Oh, and why's that?"

"Because," I whispered. Here went nothing. "I got her out of hers."

He jerked his head up. His eyes locked on mine, and I could practically feel the tension leave his body. "I don't know. We have to get Viera in a bit and check in on Ben, magically make good-tasting cupcakes out of air and water..."

"Rip." I put my hand on his shoulder and squeezed. "Live a little."

I didn't finish my thought.

I wanted to say, *Live a little—because they no longer can.*

Instead I let the unspoken words hang between us.

I didn't need to say them. We both felt them daily. The fact that we were in the grocery store arguing, teasing, wondering how the hell we were going to make cupcakes. That wasn't supposed to be our future. But it was our reality now, not theirs, and if doing something silly and immature helped Rip get out of the rut he was in and helped us bury the hatchet and live the way Monica and Brooks couldn't, then I was all for it. I just needed my partner in crime.

I'd almost given up hope that he was going to say yes when he held out his hand and said, "If I win, you have to do bedtime prep."

I grinned and took his hand in mine.

An electrical current passed between our palms, one so strong that I let out a little gasp as he squeezed, only to drop my hand seconds later like it was on fire.

He cleared his throat. "So how do we do this?"

I gave him a sly smile. "Ready. Set—"

"Wait, so I just grab stuff? What are the rules? We need rules."

"No." I grinned. "Sometimes you don't need any rules. Meet up front in ten minutes." I leaned in toward him and whispered, "Go."

He took off with his cart like a car was chasing him.

I took off with mine with a burst of laughter followed by laser-like focus. Monica had been competitive, but I'd never really seen that side of Rip before. I suddenly needed to win at all costs as I sped down the dairy aisle, grabbing what I needed and double-checking the recipe on my phone before going toward the medicine section.

What would be awkward?

I mean, I had soy-free chocolate chips in my cart, a few random ingredients including this weird gluten-free, grain-free flour that probably tasted like death.

Our cupcakes better kick ass, since the stupid flour cost triple what normal flour cost. And was this even a thing? Could there be that many allergies in one class?

I moved my cart into the medicine section and found exactly what I was looking for.

K-Y.

The warming kind.

It was awkward enough that I knew Rip would probably blush, which made me bite my lip and think dirty thoughts that had no business being in my brain since he was more attracted to cleaning products and math than he was to me.

Not true, a voice whispered. *He almost kissed me.*

I wanted to believe it.

But I couldn't, at least not yet. Maybe I just didn't want to give myself hope after everything he'd said a few minutes ago.

Yes, we'd had a few "moments," but that meant

nothing in the grand scheme of things. My heart was trying to protect me while my brain was trying to be logical, saying I had a better shot with Banks. I didn't want Banks, though. I wanted the guy who scowled more than he smiled, the one who'd just decided to do a grocery cart race in honor of his sister—and the one who was going to beat my ass if I didn't move faster!

I dropped the K-Y into my cart and then moved to the next aisle, where I grabbed some adult diapers and a plunger.

I mean... I wanted to win.

I grinned to myself. What if we upped the stakes? What if we had to purchase each other's things? He was all about rules, after all, and throwing this one at him might just send him over the edge, plus it would be hilarious.

I was still laughing when I cruised to the front of the store where Rip was waiting, his smile casual, his stance tense.

"Hey," I said, out of breath. "You ready for this?"

"Yup." He grinned.

"Cool." I started to grab his cart, but he pulled it back.

"Wait, what are you doing?"

"Improvising." I smirked. "I buy your items, you buy

189

mine. Bet I win and—" I stopped talking as I took in his cart.

Yes, he had the milk...

But he also had...

Baby oil.

A lot of baby oil.

And then...

Wart remover.

And hemorrhoid cream.

"Hey, you grabbed more than three," I pointed out.

"It's a bonus." He grinned. "The condoms just felt right." He slowly pushed the cart toward me. "Enjoy."

I wanted to immediately go back and add more items to my cart as he pulled it over and laughed. "Aw, adult diapers. Hey, these are actually useful if you jump on a trampoline, or so I've been told. I'm not a woman, so maybe you try them out, yeah?"

I was murdering him.

"Oh, cute, you got lubricant. Which of course every sexually active person needs," he said. He wasn't blushing. He was actually having...fun?

Backfire! Backfire! my brain yelled as I actually started to blush.

I was going to get in a fight in the grocery store

parking lot, wasn't I? Over oil? My cheeks burned with embarrassment as he just kept casually talking.

"Hey." He picked up the plunger. "We needed one of these. Ben's been really trying to clog every toilet in the house."

I glared. "You're not even a little bit embarrassed, are you?"

"Nope." His smile was gorgeous. "I mean, necessity is necessity. Thanks for thinking of the kids. Are you embarrassed?"

"No," I lied, holding my head up high. "This was supposed to be about having fun and letting go!"

"That's what I thought." He laughed, which made my competitive side want to crawl out, and then I realized we were together. Laughing. At the grocery store. And it wasn't awkward—I mean, apart from the items. And he wasn't scowling at me.

I wasn't plotting his death.

I was having fun with him.

A first.

And I found that I didn't want it to end. I wanted to cry party foul and play all over again if only he'd laugh like that, smile at me like that, make me feel like I was the only woman in the world.

He smiled and held out his hand toward the conveyor belt. "Shall we?"

I sighed. "I can't believe I'm buying condoms, hemorrhoid cream, wart remover, and baby oil. Never took you for the sexually adventurous type," I joked.

He grabbed my arm and pulled me against his chest, shocking me so much that it was suddenly hard to breathe. What had gotten into him?

"That's because you don't really know me...do you?" he whispered, confirming that he at least felt something too and that I wasn't wrong about the almost-kiss or any other moment.

His fingers danced along my skin before he pulled away. I turned around to face him, and our eyes locked as my lips parted. My breath caught in my chest as he took a step forward.

And I literally had a daydream of him tossing me onto the conveyor belt next to the gum and pulling my shirt off over my head.

Baby oil?

Hell yes, I'll use that oil, please and thank you.

His hand lifted like he was going to touch my face.

"Hey, you gonna pay or what?" Some high school boy with black-rimmed glasses interrupted whatever the hell was just about to happen.

"Y-yes." I somehow managed to get my debit card out of my purse. It took me three times to get the stupid chip in the chip reader.

"Hey, you OK?" the kid at checkout asked. "Your cheeks just got bright red."

"Yup. Good. Awesome. We should go." I quickly purchased the items and ignored the odd look from the high school–age cashier as he bagged my order, then quickly did Rip's.

Rip grinned as he checked out his items and said, "Thanks for your help."

Ugh.

When we got back to the car, we were both silent, and then he laughed. "That was fun."

"What's the baby oil for?" I blurted out. "Sorry, my imagination is the devil."

His eyes flashed as he leaned in and whispered, "Trade secret, can't tell."

I gasped. "Do you have a kinky side I don't know about? Tell me everything! Leave out no details!"

He burst out laughing. "Nope, no details, just know, oil can be...fun."

"Like slip-and-slide fun?" I had to ask.

His eyes darkened. "There is sliding involved."

A shiver ran through my entire body as he put the

car in drive, and for the rest of the night, even through dinner with two kids, all I could think about was sliding.

Sliding with Rip.

And our bodies sliding against each other.

And I could have sworn he knew it too, because before I went to bed, he left a bottle of oil outside my door with a note that said, "Sweet dreams."

If that was how he wanted to play it.

Game. On.

I wasn't surprised when I brushed my teeth before bed and saw my reflection in the mirror.

Flushed.

Excited.

Yeah, that plan had definitely backfired. There I'd been, arrogantly thinking I was going to help him get outside his crabby shell—and he'd thrown my world off its axis and made it so all I thought about was him— and the sides he'd never shown me.

Until tonight.

SIXTEEN

Rip

Monday it was my turn to go to work, and although there was a lot of chaos at the house, something pinched in my chest at the breakfast table.

The night before with Colby had been fun. More than fun. I hadn't been able to stop smiling like a lunatic the rest of the night, even when Colby busted out Candy Land for everyone to play before bed and teased me relentlessly about losing a kids' game.

I still smiled.

The kids thought it was hilarious that Uncle Rip didn't know how to effectively get through the Lollipop Woods.

"Uncle Rip," Ben laughed. "That's not how you do it!"

"OK, Candy Land master." I glared. "Then show me how."

"Easy." He laughed.

Colby joined in and winked at me as Ben did just that. He won twice before I was ready to look up game hacks online.

"OK, no more teasing Uncle Rip about losing," Colby scolded. "Kids, go brush your teeth while we put the game away."

"Awwww." Complaints were heard as the kids stomped up the stairs.

"No fairs!" Viera said at the top.

Colby and I both said back in unison, "Fair. It's no fair," then shared a look, our hands colliding across Licorice Lagoon.

Our fingers barely grazed, but she didn't pull back—neither did I. The room got smaller, my ability to breathe was nonexistent. Something was shifting, not just between us but with the entire family dynamic.

As if suddenly this was real.

It had felt like we were playing house, and doing it all wrong, but now it felt...right. It felt like everything I'd ever wanted with the least likely person by my side.

"Uncle Rip!" Viera wailed from the top of the stairs. "Stu pooped in my room!"

"Damn it, Stu." I grunted and jumped to my feet. "He knows he has a litter box, right?"

"Ben," Colby called up. "Did you close the laundry room door again?"

Tense quiet and then, "Maybe."

"Then you clean the poop!" she called. "Stu needs access to his box, buddy."

"Aww, man." Grumble, grumble. "I hate cat poop."

"Then keep the door open, sweetie." Colby grinned and turned to me. Our hands were no longer touching, but I had this sudden urge to just toss everything from the board and tackle her to the ground.

Over cat poop?

Good parenting?

The fact that her cheeks were still flushed from earlier?

"Colby." My voice cracked. "I'm—"

"—Uncle Rip, I need help." Ben suddenly appeared at the top of the stairs. "I forget how to clean."

Colby sighed. "Just like he forgot how to put on his pants because he didn't want to go to school."

I sighed and got to my feet. "Exactly."

"I'll clean up." Colby shrugged. "We should go to bed anyway."

Yeah, we should.

I almost voiced it out loud.

What the hell was she doing to me?

"Y-yeah. You're right..."

"Uncle Rip." Ben waved a hand in front of my face. "Are you OK? You're smiling really hard at your coffee."

"That's because Uncle Rip loves his coffee." Colby was a walking zombie and looked over at me like she was plotting something.

I chuckled again.

"Maybe he marry it," Viera said loudly, causing me to start choking.

"His coffee?" Ben made a face. "Eww, everyone knows you marry a person, duh."

"You mean!" Viera stuck out her tongue.

I continued sipping my coffee and caught the gross little dragon Viera favored with my right hand as Ben threw it at her head. "No toys at the table," I reminded them.

"Uhhhh, that's not fair! She gets her dragon, but I can't have my Legos?"

I made a grand show of setting the dragon on the chair so it wasn't actually at the table, then felt the need to tell him Legos were totally different.

Colby and I were convinced they weren't toys but a government experiment to see how small and painful to step on it could make them before you decided to burn them all.

"Though...," I added. "Technically a stuffed animal is more or less like a blanket you carry to make you feel better."

"My Legos make me feel better." He chomped on a bite of Cheerios as milk dripped down his chin.

Touché.

Colby gave me a look that basically said, *Don't you dare give in, even though he's super cute.*

I smiled.

Her cheeks went bright pink, and I found that I had a really hard time looking away—that is, until Viera let out a shriek. "SPIDER!"

Colby immediately went into action. "Where's the little bastard?"

"Swear jar!" Ben singsonged.

"Th-here!" Viera jabbed her finger in my direction.

I froze and pointed at myself. "On me?"

"By yours feets!" Viera wailed. "Right in the middle."

"It's frozen in fear." Colby nodded, a crazed look in her blue eyes. "I'm killing it."

"Just don't kill me," I reminded her. "Remember, your survival depends on my ability to breathe."

"What makes you say that?" Colby said as she grabbed a magazine and rolled it up, then started to slowly make her way toward me.

"Two kids. One parent. You tell me," I whispered.

"Fair point." She raised the magazine and smacked it down between my legs and looked up at me triumphantly. "Dead."

"No it's not," I said.

"Huh? What?"

"It's on your arm." I pointed.

"Then get it off!" she wailed, shaking both arms in the air like she was going to take flight. "Rip!"

"Stop moving!" I grabbed her right arm and swatted the spider away. Ben grabbed a yellow Lego and took care of the rest. "Always knew Legos killed."

"Now we have proof," Colby whispered, her voice quivering.

I hadn't realized we were so close until she spoke, until I looked down and noticed I was holding her and she wasn't pulling away. Just like the night before.

"Sorry." She licked her lips but didn't move other than that, just stared up at me, eyes searching.

"At least we both survived." My voice was deep, like I was minutes away from growling and carrying her upstairs over my shoulder, then slamming the door and announcing, *Mine!*

Her body was soft against me, her hair a mess, but I liked it. Why did I suddenly like the mess?

Why did I suddenly like *her* so much she consumed my every waking thought? So much that I didn't want to go to work and I loved work. But suddenly all I wanted to do was stay with her and kill spiders.

I cleared my throat. "I should be going."

"Yeah." She started to pull away.

"Stu, nooo!" Ben yelled. "Out! Out!"

We broke apart quickly as Colby managed to grab the cat and pat the back of his head.

"No, Stu!" Ben started to sob. "He's choking on the spider!"

"You're gonna have to put your hands inside his mouth and pull it out!" Colby held up the cat to me as its legs dangled. It kept coughing, its eyes watering.

With a muffled curse I reached two fingers into Stu's mouth and pulled out a crumpled-up, soggy brown spider.

Amazing.

And it was only Monday.

Colby burst out laughing as I dropped the spider into the trash can and carried the cat over to Ben. "He's fine, bud."

He wiped his nose and sniffled. "Dad got me Stu."

I shared a knowing look with Colby, then leaned down on my haunches. "Do you want to talk about your dad? Sometimes it helps to talk about the people we're missing." I was taking a page from Colby's book and hoping it would help.

"No." He shrugged. "I talk to him every night."

I swallowed the lump in my throat. "What do you guys talk about?"

He shrugged. "Dumb stuff like how Stu's doing, Viera's dolls, my spelling tests, the time you got kicked out of my jujitsu match—"

I shot a glare at Colby when she snorted behind her hand.

"Oh, and how I pray every night for you and Aunt Colby to get married so we can be a family again."

Colby froze.

Viera ignored us as she started playing with the damn dragon on the counter, or at least I thought she was ignoring us until she piped up, "That's cool, Ben, I pray that too. 'Member they cuddle."

Thank God my phone started buzzing in my pocket and someone knocked on the door because I didn't know how to respond to that. This was all so new, and the way Colby and I were interacting felt like there was something growing between us, something we both wanted. But how would that even happen? How did parents who were actually married even navigate a relationship with kids around? My heart broke and my chest hurt. I had no answers for them, not when I didn't even have any answers for myself.

"Hey, talk to your dad anytime you want, bud." I ruffled his hair and kissed him and Viera on the forehead, then approached Colby while the knocking intensified at the door.

"Have a good day," she whispered.

"You too." I awkwardly stepped forward and pulled her in for a lame hug, then hesitated, only to have Colby give me a quick hug that I wanted to last a hell of a lot longer than two seconds. The knocking intensified.

"Coming," I finally yelled, and I went to the door, jerking it open.

Heather stood there with a cup of coffee in one hand and a small bag in the other, her smile widening as she looked me up and down. "I'm surprised, no ketchup or Cheerios present."

Why did that feel like an insult? And why was she suddenly coming by when she knew I'd see her at work?

"Is there something wrong at the office?" I asked, frowning.

"Not at all." She shrugged. "I was just in the neighborhood and decided to drop off some much needed caffeine and food for you—it's a quinoa breakfast bur-rito with turkey sausage!"

I could imagine Colby getting stabby eyes behind me. She was a food blogger; while she couldn't cook worth shit, she sure as hell knew her food.

"Thanks." I took the food and coffee and then looked over my shoulder.

Colby had gone still, her face pale as Heather looped an arm in mine. "I Ubered here, why don't we ride together to work?"

I'd always imagined myself with a woman like Heather, and we'd even gone on a date forever ago, but there hadn't been any spark. At least not for me. And I'd thought not for Heather either. So why was she here?

"Have a good day!" Heather waved at everyone with a happy smile, and then we were shutting the door, and I was feeling like a weak-ass human.

Why was I even letting her lead me anywhere?

I shook my arm away. "We aren't dating anymore, remember?"

Her face fell a bit, her eyes narrowing. "Oh, sorry, I was just being friendly. Besides, just like we aren't dating, it's not like those are your kids, and you've been doing nothing but spending time here."

I saw red. "It's been less than a month since their parents died, and you want to bring that up now?"

Her face fell. "I didn't mean anything bad. I'm just saying this is temporary, this whole...pretend-family thing. It will be easier for you to process that now rather than later. You know, once you jump back into the dating scene again, get your own place, it will be super easy to share custody and all."

She sighed and waited at the passenger door, oblivious to the anger I had simmering beneath the surface.

I calmly opened the door for her and then walked around and got in behind the wheel.

We drove in silence.

I gripped the steering wheel like I wanted to pull it free and toss it out the window, and she texted as if this were her future.

By my side.

In my expensive car.

That future flashed before my eyes. Society events with her well-connected family, moving to a mansion, nannies.

Everything that had seemed normal—even achievable—at one point, and now, I wanted the mess.

I wanted the chaos.

I wanted ketchup on my shirt because it meant that I'd been enjoying a meal with Ben or Viera.

I wanted the sleepless nights because they meant I was comforting them.

I wanted the crazy.

Not the easy.

Heather put her hand on my thigh. "I'm so glad things are going to get back to normal soon. I was talking to my parents and thought it would be good to set up a dinner. Just the four of us, what do you think? For old times' sake? They really miss you...I do too, you haven't been the same since everything, a little away time will be good."

"I think I'm still your boss, so unless they want me to do their taxes...," I joked, hoping she'd take the hint.

"Oh, I thought I told you. They fired their accountant last week, sorry, you haven't really been in a ton, so it must have slipped my mind." She examined her nails. "They want to hand over the Miller Enterprises account to your firm. Great news, right?"

I nearly choked.

"I think right now it's worth around...a hundred and fifty million, give or take? I mean, obviously you'd need to be exclusively *their* accountant, but I'll let Dad handle those details. They'll give you a signing bonus and make sure you're very taken care of. It will be like..." She paused. "Like you're part of the family."

I couldn't believe what I was hearing.

"See ya inside," Heather said as she opened the door. "I'll look at your schedule and see when you're free for dinner or maybe even brunch?" She leaned over and kissed my cheek before getting out of the car and slamming the door.

I grabbed my coffee, left the weird quinoa burrito, and followed her into the building. I made my way to my office, only to retrace my steps and knock on Banks's door.

"Hey." He didn't look up. "You never stop at my door." He smiled like he knew what I was going to ask as he took in my coffee and the rage on my face.

Heather chose that moment to walk by and grin. "Oh, good, you're finishing off your coffee, I'm just grabbing your schedule now."

I opened my mouth.

Closed it.

Stared at Banks harder, then closed the door behind me.

"Gonna stop you before you make an ass out of yourself trying to explain your feelings when I already know what they are. Yes, you like Colby, yes, Heather's a social-climbing psychopath that you've entrusted to help run your firm, and finally—" He took a deep breath. "Would I date Colby? Yes. I would jump at the chance. She's hilarious, she's full of life, she's my perfect match like that stupid MTV show, but I also know the heart wants what it wants, so what should you do? Glad you asked. You go home tonight and you kiss her. That's it, no speeches needed, no grand gesture, you pull her into your arms and you do what you've been dying to do ever since you got pissed off at the movie theater and almost killed me dead."

"But—"

"Oh, and make it a good kiss, not like this controlled let-me-only-give-ten-percent-tongue-just-in-case kiss. Girls like Colby? They want to be picked up and set on a counter, they want you to push them up against a wall, pull their hair." He started tugging at his shirt. "Sorry. That just got weird. Anyway, point is, don't be such a chickenshit and listen to your best friend."

I shook my head. "I'll at least admit you're a good friend..."

Banks's head jerked up. "I knew I'd wear you down." He smiled. "As for Brooks, he would have encouraged this entire scenario. Some might say he inspired me."

"To go after the woman I wanted," I grumbled. "I

could just see him sitting in the back of the theater with Monica, laughing their asses off."

"Affirmative. Because you're blind as shit," he pointed out. "And because I know you, remember? Monica always said you needed more of a shove instead of a point in the right direction, and I figured shoving would help you see what all of us have seen for years."

My chest tightened. "And what's that?"

"You need to stop controlling the world around you—and stop worrying about the life you've always wanted, especially since it's been in front of you all this time. Want to know what Monica told me a week before she died?"

I walked slowly toward his desk and pulled out a chair. "I don't know. Do I?"

He leaned forward. "Me, Monica, and Brooks were all out for drinks, and I think you were working late. She was telling me about Colby and the disastrous date you guys went on, and I laughed and said, 'That's exactly what stick-up-his-ass needs.'"

"Hey!"

"And Monica? She just smiled and said, 'One day it's going to happen. I can feel it. One day, she'll be his family.' Obviously it happened in a horrifying way, but I know, in my soul, that she'd be happy that you and

Colby are together, that you're following your heart, and dude, if you start crying, I'm gonna start crying, and I have an image to uphold, so just say thank you, shake my hand, make a grunting noise, and walk out of my office. Do some math or something..."

"Math." I laughed out loud, and then I couldn't stop. Maybe it was the stress or just the fact that I'd been an idiot, but I laughed, he laughed, and I finally felt like some of the pressure in my chest had dissipated, like maybe the world wasn't as gray as it once had been.

Hours later I was still thinking about all those times with Colby, the almost-kisses, the stares, the hugs, and it was killing me to be stuck at my desk. When had that ever happened in my entire life? I was a complete workaholic.

I grabbed a pencil and started twirling it between my fingers.

I literally had no idea what I was even working on. I had my laptop open, papers on my desk, and nothing, absolutely nothing in my brain but kissing Colby.

A knock sounded at my door, then Banks poked his head in. "How's the focus coming along?"

I was tempted to flip him off, but instead I pointed at the door for him to leave. "I have a lot of work to do today."

"Yes, but how much work have you actually done...
friend?" His smile was all-knowing.

"Out!" I pointed at the door again.

He held up his hands and shut the door quietly.

I stared at my laptop and took a deep breath. I was
a professional. I could do this, I could compartmentalize my work life and my home life.

Home life.

Huh, months ago I would have laughed at the possibility, even though I'd always wanted it.

Now I had it.

What the hell was I even doing at work right now?

When I could be home?

When I could pick up Ben from school? Or make
horrible cupcakes? How did parents even do this regu-
larly without getting stressed out?

Wine?

Working out?

Yoga?

I groaned and pinched my nose, then grabbed my
phone and stared too hard at the screen, finally decid-
ing to send a text.

Me:

> How did the cupcakes go
> over?

Colby:

A kid cried, so yeah super well thanks for asking!

Me:

Oh God, because they tasted so bad?

Colby:

I prefer to think of the glass as half full, clearly they were so good he wanted more. Thus the tears.

Me:

I like it.

Colby:

How's work?

Me:

I think I'd prefer a cupcake.

Colby:

What about a breakfast burrito with quinoa? I know what quinoa is!

I laughed.

Me:

I know you do, food is literally your job, too bad you can't cook, you could have been a killer chef.

Colby:

> I prefer to eat the hard work, not prepare it.

Me:

> That's fair.

Colby:

> Oh man, Viera just got up from her nap, shit, where's her dragon? She said Ben hid it before school and I can't find it anywhere!

I thought long and hard about it.

Me:

> Check his Lego stash.

I drummed my fingertips against my desk in impatience, only to have her ping back right away with a picture of the damn dragon captioned "EUREKA!"

Colby:

> How did you know he'd hide it in his Legos?

Me:

> All men think alike…

Colby:

> I'll just take your word for it, oh shoot, gotta run, it's the scary cry and dinner isn't ready and…maybe stay at work for a few extra hours so I don't—shit gotta go!

What? I thought our text exchange had gone well. Now she wanted me to work late? I frowned down at my phone, then looked back up at my computer and shook my head. Not a chance in hell.

I was going home.

SEVENTEEN

Colby

I heard the front door shut with a soft click—but it might as well have been a nuclear bomb going off. After several arguments over nap time earlier, I'd finally gotten the kids to go lay down for quiet time though by the looks of the house anyone would think a war had broken out before I was able to successfully accomplish anything past attempting to keep my calm before rocking in the corner with a bottle of wine clutched in one hand and a pillow to scream into in the other.

Tears and flour caked my cheeks as I furiously rubbed them in an effort to look presentable. I sprinted into the kitchen, nearly taking out my right hip against the cold, hard granite countertop.

Pain throbbed in cadence with my panicked heart as a car door slammed—his car door.

Great. We were literally back to square one. I could see

it now. Especially after this morning with our moment and his stupid assistant stopping by. He was going to be all anal again, and I was going to have to explain myself.

Why were things like this between us? It felt like Rip had changed so much in the past few weeks, but I knew in my soul the minute he saw this chaos he was going to lose his mind, yell, possibly tell me I was immature, and then I would cry.

"No, no, no," I whispered to myself as I quickly shoved all the cookies that weren't burned farther onto the counter while dumping the others into the trash. Along with the leftover flour, several cups of purple glitter slime Viera had decided she had to make, and an indistinguishable brown putty that I hoped to God wasn't from the old grumpy cat were scattered all over the place in green Solo cups, making it look like a college frat house instead of a madhouse. Stu meowed at me and gave me a look that said he was about two seconds away from puking up a hairball again, and don't even get me started on a cat that needed diapers half the time because life made him "anxious."

The whole spider scenario earlier today wasn't helping matters either. What cat eats a spider, then chokes on it? A shudder rocked my body.

"Shoo!" I tried to shove the cat away from the table he'd just jumped on, only to groan when he knocked another two cups full of slime onto the hardwood floor.

Footsteps sounded.

Stu abandoned me.

And the house still looked horrific.

Panic flared in my chest, and suddenly all I could do was stand there and watch in horror as Rip rounded the corner in his pristine black slacks and ironed navy shirt. Not a dark wavy piece of jet-black hair was out of place. His green eyes locked onto mine and twitched.

Both of them, not just one, both simultaneously. How was that even physically possible?

His height dominated the dirty kitchen, making me feel small—and stupid, always stupid. He didn't say a word to make me feel that way—he didn't need to. His barely controlled rage said it all.

Failure.

I was a failure as a mom.

And at present, he was there to witness my failings.

Again.

After our pact two weeks before, things had been better between us, but I knew that this? This mess would be the final straw for him.

He understood the chaos—after all, he hadn't escaped our pact unscathed when we swapped roles—but he was still better at multitasking than I was.

I wanted to yell that it wasn't supposed to be this way.

I wanted to point my finger at him and tell him that he was half to blame, that we were never supposed to be put in this position.

That life wasn't fair, and God hadn't blessed me with one domestic bone in my body—and truthfully, I was ready to say that, all of that and more, because I was exhausted, and unlike Rip I wasn't perfect, I didn't understand the word *control*, any more than I could understand French.

I opened my mouth and closed it as a blue bucket next to his feet came into view. Somehow the cat had knocked it over. Water and slime now pooled in front of him, inches from the toes of his perfect shoes. With what we'd used to create the slime, which just so happened to be loads and loads of soap, I knew his perfectly polished shoes with no traction were going to take one step and slip.

"Wait!" I held out both hands.

His green eyes narrowed in on me, and then he

slowly took in the rest of the dirty kitchen with a look of pure horror and disbelief. "Did we get robbed?"

I glared. "Yes, and all they wanted to do was bake cookies and make slime—weirdest robbers ever, but don't worry, I'm sure the cops can figure things out by the very chaotic crime scene left over." I finished with a muttered "jackass" under my breath; OK, so maybe it was less of a mutter and more of a verbal attack, but still. Come on!

He let out an exhausted sigh as the muscles of his forearms flexed, drawing my attention to his rolled-up sleeves and slightly tired look. Maybe, just maybe his day had been as hard as mine. "Look, I don't want to fight again."

I deflated a bit. This was new to both of us. Why couldn't we just get along? I hung my head and mentally waved the white flag. "Me neither, it's been a long day."

He sighed in exhaustion, or maybe it was envy. Then again, I could be going crazy. "At least you were home."

And I was murdering him in his sleep—or at least holding a pillow over his face in a threatening manner until he understood the threat. It didn't matter that he had at least forty pounds of muscle on me. I was scrappy and pissed and could easily sleep for a year straight.

He took another step.

"No, wait—"

Of course he didn't listen, which meant the minute his foot hit the mystery substance, his leg went one way and he went another.

Arms flailing, he slipped into the water and slime, then fell with a thump onto his ass. His briefcase went flying out of his hand. Papers went flying out of his briefcase, scattering like snow. And because I'm the unluckiest person in the world, that same briefcase hit the remaining Solo cups on the counter as well as the last flour bowl, sending it over his head with a whoosh and a final crack of doom as it hit the floor.

I hurried over without thinking. "Are you OK? I was trying to warn you and—"

I went tumbling onto his lap, butt pointing at his chin, hands bracing his thighs like I was ready to pounce. I quickly flipped around but still somehow ended up straddling him. Our heads nearly knocked as he wiped his face and glared.

"S-sorry."

"Slime?" He tilted his head like he was curious,

which made me pause; he didn't have a curious bone in his body.

"I was a scientist in another life," I offered lamely, trying to control my breathing. Did he have to be so attractive? So annoying? So perfect?

Lately things had been strained between us, with this weird heaviness that spoke of things neither of us was admitting to, especially after both kids got the flu and ended up in one giant bed between us, barricading them in as if we were physically trying to protect them from the world—that was our job now, right?

"Purple glitter, though? Really?"

At least he wasn't yelling. Then again, he never raised his voice. Sometimes I wished he would. Sometimes I wished he'd just react, one time in his life. And I wished that he would mourn.

He hadn't cried yet or broken down.

The funeral had been a blur, though—a blur I refused to focus on since he was still giving me a strange look I couldn't decipher. The flour made him look ridiculous but more approachable.

"What?" I didn't move.

"Your eyes." He licked his lips as pieces of flour fell between our bodies. "I forgot how blue they are up close."

I fought hard not to stare down at his plump, wet lip, at the way his tongue had snuck out.

His lips were beautiful, full, a complete masterpiece of masculine beauty paired with a harshness that almost warned mere mortals to look away.

Something about the intense closeness broke me, made me want to get closer, made me need his comfort more than my next breath. I leaned in, expecting him to back away like he always did or make an excuse or remind me of his vow to never touch me for as long as we both shall live.

But this time, he cradled the sides of my face with wet hands.

This time, our foreheads touched on a rough exhalation.

This time, Rip Edison leaned forward and pressed a painfully slow kiss to my lips.

My breath caught as he deepened the kiss, tasting me like I was a chocolate sample he wanted to devour, and then as soon as I wrapped my arms around his neck the sound of a small cry filled the air.

We quickly broke apart.

"Not it!" we declared in unison.

EIGHTEEN

Colby

Dinner was a bit tense as I attempted to make something that resembled actual food without burning the house down. I was still thinking about the kiss, about what all these feelings and moments between us meant. The only answer I'd landed on was that all this thinking was not improving my cooking skills. I'd been trying my ass off, but I still trusted DoorDash more than my own cooking, and by the looks on the kids' faces, so did they. I'd spent my adult life going to fancy restaurants, writing about the food, the resort or hotel experience, the nightlife, rooms, amenities. My job was to travel and comment on all of it, so in that time, I'd never had the desire to cook since my job was to literally eat, drink, and be merry before lying down in a fluffy clean bed with chocolate on my pillow.

I sighed. That was nice. Or had been nice.

And now this. I looked down at the chicken that the kids were attempting to chew.

It was kind of dry.

The potatoes needed ketchup.

And the green beans were...well, green beans.

The sound of utensils scraping plates put me on edge, as I had my laptop open in a vain attempt to get my next article done. But after more commentary on my cooking, where Rip said yum and the kids said yuck, I finally decided to take some pictures of them instead of working on my post.

I'd do that later.

At least I'd have content for my Instagram.

I took a shot of Viera making a face. Then Ben holding up a green bean with his fork and frowning as if he were confused about whether it was a vegetable or unsafe to eat.

I laughed.

Rip joined in, and by the time I was done, I had an entire quick little photo post that still met my quota for the week even though I still had to work on my other assignment for the blog.

Maybe reality would be better for my followers anyway. I had barely been posting this month on my own personal accounts, but maybe if they saw what I was working with they'd take pity or at least laugh at the messiness of my life, which used to look so perfect and amazing. Sipping martinis by the pool, eating Wagyu steak on the weekly, and working on my tan.

Why did this life suddenly feel more fulfilling, even though it was chaotic? I cleared my throat and tried not to stare stupidly at Rip and beg him with my eyes to help me overanalyze our relationship.

"Those will be good," Rip said, digging into his chicken like it didn't taste like death. I tried not to focus on his mouth or the way his lips curled into a genuine smile. I wanted so badly to ask about the kiss. About all the things that had happened this last week when it seemed like both of us had waved the white flag. But how did a person even begin to have that conversation with two sets of little ears perking up every time adult topics were introduced?

It didn't help that Ben was a wizard with words and spelling, so even if I did spell out conversations, he'd know exactly what I was talking about.

"How was your day, Viera?" Rip asked. "I saw you made some slime..."

I clutched my fork like a weapon.

"Yes! We's had so fun!" Viera laughed. "And Aunt Colby got messy!"

"Shocker," I said mostly to myself with a laugh.

"Sometimes messy is good," Rip said softly, looking over at me before looking back at Viera. "Especially when it puts that smile on your face, sweetheart."

"Then I so messy too!" Viera started laughing and then took a bite of chicken. "So good, Aunt Colby!" She swallowed and then shoved her chair back. "All done."

"Viera." I crossed my arms. "Two more bites."

She pouted and then shoved them into her mouth and tried through chews to say, "Can, I watch, *PAW Patrol*? Pweeeeease!"

"Ask Uncle Rip." Ha ha, sucker.

He gave me a nice-one look and pulled Viera into his lap. Her little arms wrapped around his neck, and then he was whispering something into her ear. She perked up, and he put her on her feet.

She came sprinting toward me, jumped into my arms, and whispered, "I love you mostest. Thank yous for dinner."

And then she was running up the stairs. Meanwhile, Ben was eating another piece of chicken and groaning as he shoved more food into his mouth. "I think I'm full."

An hour from now he'd ask for a peanut butter and jelly sandwich, I'd bet my life on it, but I let it slide.

"Go brush your teeth. You can have twenty minutes of screen time, then bed."

He slumped out of his chair and slowly went up the stairs.

I smiled after him. "They're so different, but they both have so much of Brooks and Monica in them. It's really nice to watch." I shrugged. "As much as I wish they were here to see how much those little boogers are growing—I'm glad we get to at least experience it for them." *Do not cry. Don't cry!*

"Ben would eat his plate if we didn't stop him." Rip stood and started clearing the table with a sad smile. "And Viera just wants to give the world a hug."

I grinned in agreement. "They're adorable. Exhausting, but adorable. How was, um..." I casually grabbed some glasses and made my way toward the sink. "You know, um...work, after Heather stopped by and... stuff."

"And stuff"? Really?

He was quiet. Too quiet. Why was I freaking out? He seemed calm, not like he was ready to tell me bad news, but insecurity flared up like always.

She really was perfect for him on paper.

Ugh, why had I even mentioned her?

Why did I care?

I mean, I didn't care—much.

OK, I cared a lot.

He'd kissed me.

Me.

But maybe it had been an impulse? Or maybe I was just being ridiculous and the chicken was affecting my brain cells.

"She's been acting weird" was all he said. Maybe my gut instinct had been right and she was just being the same mean girl I used to go to school with, the one who would do anything to nail the popular guy and keep him for herself.

Besides.

He'd kissed me.

Maybe if I just kept repeating it, I'd finally believe that it was possible Rip had feelings for me, real feelings.

Things had shifted between us so much in the last week, and after that kiss...my entire body felt like I was going to do something stupid any minute, like kiss him again or just accidentally slip while doing dishes and collapse against him to see if he caught me. Yeah, bad idea. Stupid idea.

Or the best idea ever?

"What do you mean 'weird'?" I asked, moving

dishes toward the sink and trying to act as nonchalant as possible.

How was he acting so normal after kissing me?

"Heather"—I couldn't tell his mood by the way he said her name—"was...just...strange today. We had a talk in the car, and I'm starting to think that working for me might not be the best fit for her, you know? I wouldn't worry too much about it. Something just seems...off."

I nearly dropped the plate I was holding as I shakily brought it to the sink. "Did she do something illegal?"

"No." He barked out a laugh. "Nothing illegal."

"Did she...do something wrong?" I was totally reaching, but I was curious about what she'd done in all her perfection to make him even contemplate letting her go or having that conversation. It clearly wasn't the burrito or the coffee. I was being obsessive about it, needy for details because I knew it would at least help me understand where he was at.

"She does everything right, but that's not the point. Maybe doing everything right means you're wrong, and clearly I'm exhausted." He shrugged it off. "Honestly, I don't want to talk about it or work." He walked toward the sink, his hand brushing my hip like he meant to do it. I tensed and looked up at him. His eyes locked on mine with an intensity that my poor heart needed. His look said, *It's not her.*

Weird how a look can do that. I swallowed my nerves and attempted to act as normal as possible.

I clutched the plate and started vigorously scrubbing it clean, not even realizing that he'd come up behind me. He put his hands in the dish soap, helping me stroke across the ceramic, and apparently I wasn't just cleaning it off for the dishwasher, I was going to stay in that spot forever, with that plate, and with him behind me.

Back and forth, back and forth. He held my hands firm, his body pressed up against my back. "She made an offer I had to refuse."

"O-oh?" I swallowed. "What was that?"

"A perfectly boring life where Legos don't exist."

"I thought you wanted a perfectly boring life where Legos don't exist." Throat suddenly dry, heart pounding, I tried to focus on the dish and nothing but the dish, but he was close, so close, and the kiss was still fresh in my mind, as was her invading our family space earlier.

"Yeah, well..." His lips grazed my ear. "Things change. It was a hard day only because I had a lot of thinking to do and had an extremely difficult time doing so."

"Hope you didn't strain a brain cell," I teased nervously. I was so going to drop a plate and kill the moment.

"Nah, I'm feeling pretty strong right now," he snapped right back, his lips grazing my neck in a kiss that had my entire body shuddering with delight.

"What are you doing?" I asked quietly, afraid of rejection, afraid of acceptance, just afraid of everything as he spun me in his arms and started kissing me.

My hands were wet from dish soap.

I had bubbles on my shirt, slime probably still in my hair.

And Rip didn't care.

He kissed me hard, his tongue sliding past my lips, taking control of how deeply he was kissing me as I arched up against him, my arms sliding around his neck as he pulled me up onto the counter next to the sink and wrapped my legs around his waist.

He was hard where I was soft.

He was clearly aroused.

I needed more of his taste.

His touch.

Everything seemed to click into place in one messy moment.

Maybe that was how it was always supposed to be.

"Uncle Rip!" Ben yelled downstairs. "We're ready for bed!"

"Me too." Rip's eyes sparkled as he kissed me one last time. "Me too."

"Someone's being spontaneous."

"Someone found that stick up his ass and burned it."

"Painful."

"Necessary."

"Better?"

He nipped at my lips again. "You have no idea."

I groaned, jerking him by the shirt to meet his lips, and then, "Aunt Colby! I's ready for bed story!"

Viera.

Our foreheads touched.

"Duty calls," he rasped.

"Yeah." I didn't want to leave. What if I was dreaming? What if this moment was just a mistake on his part? Work pressure? Bad chicken?

"Divide and conquer." He grinned. "You tell the story, I'll tuck Ben in, and then we'll come back downstairs and finish...dishes."

Was he talking about dishes? Or *dishes*?

I licked my lips, tasting him there, wanting to taste more.

His eyes fell to my mouth. "You taste..." His jaw clenched, and then he tilted his head back, looking up at the ceiling. "Let me start over, I always thought it was cliché when in movies the guy says the girl tastes like strawberries when she hasn't even eaten any, or that she tastes perfect and they just ate garlic fries. It's cheesy, it makes zero sense, and it's false advertising...but you? You taste like I imagine sunshine would taste like, warm, inviting, and then blazing hot."

I gaped. "That was weirdly sweet."

"I can be sweet." He shrugged. "Maybe I've just never had a reason to be."

"And now?" I asked.

"Uncle Ri-ip," Ben called down. "You're taking foreverrrrrrrr."

"Now?" Rip smiled. "I'm being summoned."

"Ignore him, he'll eventually fall asleep or just yell himself hoarse. I mean, aren't there more important things, like finishing this conversation?" I smiled back.

"Tastes good and she's tempting. Didn't see you coming, Colby...and that's the truth."

I wanted to dissect every single sentence that had just come out of his mouth. Unfortunately, Ben showed up at the top of the stairs, his little knobby knees making me laugh as he crossed his arms over his chest and pouted. "Adults are slow."

"Yeah." I passed Rip and winked as I headed up the stairs. "They really are...the slowest."

"You'll pay for that," he said under his breath.

"Promise?" I called over my shoulder.

His eyes burned into mine.

It was our perfect moment, the one that defined the rest of our lives, I felt it in my soul.

And then I tripped on the last step and face-planted right next to Ben's feet.

"Wow, Aunt Colby, you went flying!" he pointed out. "Are you OK?"

I grunted and pressed my face against the carpet. "Might just hang out here for a bit."

Rip leaned down and whispered, "You're cute when you fall on your face..."

I jerked my head back and stared him down. "You're the worst."

"No." He held out his hand. "Now let's hurry and get the kids to bed so I can show you all the ways I'm the best, but watch out...Lego minefield ahead."

"It's like they strategically put them on the floor to get us!" I stepped over each of the Legos thinking

I'd finally made it, only to get a minuscule clear one between my toes.

I hissed, then pulled it out and held it up.

"Hey, I was looking for that one." Ben grabbed it out of my hands and went over to his Lego table and put it on his pirate ship.

"Amazing." I shook my head. "How does he even remember where they go?"

"Pffft." Ben laughed. "It's not hard."

"Or maybe you're just super-duper smart," I offered.

"That too." He giggled, and then, "VIERA, COME TO MY ROOM FOR STORY TIME!"

Rip yawned like he needed his ears to pop from the noise, earning a laugh from me and Ben as Viera came zooming into the room. "I here!"

"Someone really needs to have a discussion about volume in this house," I grumbled, eyeing Rip.

"Kids, don't yell." He smirked at me while saying it, probably well aware that I wanted to strangle him, then straddle him to the ground and kiss my way up and down his body.

"Aunt Colby? Are you OK?" Viera tugged on my shirt. "You've been staring at Uncle Rip like he's a cookie!"

My face flushed.

Rip licked his lips.

How dare he!

In front of the kids!

Damn it!

I snapped out of it. "St-story time." I sat next to Ben on the bed and pulled Viera into my lap. "There once was a princess—"

"Who found her prince," Rip said smoothly.

"But he turned out to be a frog," I added with a glare.

He crossed his arms. "Maybe the frog forgot he was a prince, which meant he had bad manners. You know, when frogs live in captivity they're seventy percent more likely to have attitude problems."

"And you one hundred percent made that up." I jabbed a finger at him.

"Google it," he challenged.

"I'm not falling for that again. Last time you told me to Google about the life expectancy of a goat after it drank its own milk and I actually did it and looked stupid!"

He pressed his lips together. "Yeah, that was hilarious."

"Goats drink their own milk?" Ben asked in a horrified voice. "Does that mean I have to drink my own milk?"

I patted his head. "Nobody's milking you, Ben."

"Where do babies get milk?" Viera asked.

"Er, so this frog..." I cleared my throat.

"Prince," Rip corrected.

I looked heavenward. "Fine, this frog prince"—I made air quotes—"finally got his head out of...his pond—"

"Nice," Rip said under his breath.

"And the princess was curious why he was suddenly so willing to breathe the fresh air and talk to her instead of stare at his own reflection in the pond and bask in his own presence."

Rip snorted. "Maybe your perception was off the whole time; maybe the frog was staring at the princess's reflection but was too scared to admit it. Maybe he was scared to admit that all he'd ever known was the pond, and she wanted him to go to a new pond, a scarier, bigger pond, and then another, and another—"

"Well, maybe he should have just grown—er—up and admitted the truth rather than make her feel like her pond was too messy."

"Her pond is messy," Rip said.

"Messy isn't bad," I countered.

He sighed. "Messy reminds the frog of chaos, and chaos, after living in that pond...it makes him scared.

237

Most frogs over the age of thirty are set in their ways, you know..."

I'd completely forgotten we were trying to tell a bedtime story, which was just as well, since I noticed that both Ben and Viera had fallen asleep in Ben's bed.

"Never thought I'd see the day where you'd be the one to bore someone to sleep...," Rip whispered.

"You helped, math wizard."

"Low blow," he growled.

I liked it.

A lot.

The rasp from his voice. The way he stared into my soul. "Did you mean it?"

"Mean what?" He slowly pulled Viera into his arms and carried her to her room. I followed behind them and waited for him in the hallway. After what seemed like a lifetime, he reappeared, shutting the door quietly behind him.

"The frog story," I blurted out. "Did you mean what you said?"

He leaned against the opposite wall, his eyes flashing. "What do you think?"

Slowly he made his way over to me, one step, two, and then pain flashed across his face.

I dodged a Lego and clapped my hand over his

mouth. "Wake them up, and I'm coming for you in your sleep!"

His eyes lit up.

"You're such a guy," I hissed.

He pulled my hand away from his mouth and kissed the inside of my wrist, then pinned me against the hallway wall. "I want you."

I stuck my chin out in a defiant gesture. "Give me one good reason why you should have me."

Maybe bad chicken also makes me confident. I wanted him to say all the right things, things I needed to hear to know that this was real. That we were real.

"Because you terrify me. You make me want to color outside of the lines, which I hate. You're an incredible aunt. You're a loyal friend. Because you're beautiful even when you're walking around with ketchup on your shirt. Because it bothers me that you don't see how unique you are, how special it is to be included in your circle. And finally because I've tasted..." He nipped at my lips. "I've drunk..." He deepened the kiss, his tongue sliding against mine. "And I fell."

I was panting from one stupid kiss. I clung to his shirt, my eyes zeroing in on his perfectly muscular chest. "I don't work out."

"I know."

"Kissing me won't stop me from annoying you ninety-nine percent of the time, you know."

"No." He kissed me again and pulled back. "But it does get you to shut the hell up."

He kissed away any protest I could have had as he lifted me into the air and carried me further down the hall.

He was taking me into his room.

Rip was kissing me and taking me into his room.

And I wasn't daydreaming.

And we weren't fighting—much.

And it felt right. Everything about that moment felt right.

So I let myself fall into it.

I let myself trust Rip.

NINETEEN

Rip

Never thought I'd see the day—or the night—that I'd hijack a story about a frog, make it about me, and use it as a way to get a woman into bed.

But here we were.

And I was doing exactly that.

My hands shook as I kicked the door closed softly and then started raining kisses down her neck as she panted my name.

Heart thudding against my chest, I guided her toward the bed, then tugged her shirt over her head and tossed it to the ground.

"Fuck." I'd forgotten how perfect her breasts were. She'd worn a bikini on a trip we'd taken to Mexico with Monica and Brooks, and I'd had to tell myself not to notice about a million times.

She smiled up at me. "I hope that's a good 'fuck.'"

"You're sexy when you swear." I reached for her; I wanted to cover her body with mine and kiss her until I had to have her or died from wanting her. "And it's a good one."

"They're a bit big." She cupped herself, making me groan.

I slapped her hands away. "You get to touch them all the time. It's my turn."

She laughed. "Yes, because that's what big-chested women do, we just sit around all day and touch our boobs."

"I like that fantasy," I growled, and my dick showed me it concurred by straining toward her. "And I wouldn't judge you if you did. You're stunning."

She swallowed slowly and looked away as if she didn't want to look me in the eyes.

I thumbed the bright-pink bra and grinned. "Look at me."

She lifted her chin. "Better?"

"How am I looking at you right now? Describe it."

She chewed her lower lip. Making a little red mark on the middle of her lower lip before she sighed. "Can't we just have sex and call it good?"

"Why?" I leaned in. "Are you scared?"

She gave me a slow nod. "What if this doesn't work, Rip? What if we have sex and then I'm horrible or you start...I don't know, doing math problems out loud because that's your kink, and then we still have to take care of the kids and live together?"

I forced a blank expression on my face. "How'd you know?"

Her entire face drained of color. "That's it? That's your move?"

"Math should always be included in moves." I grinned. "But no, I just wanted to see your face."

That at least had her smiling. "Hmmm, I sense another game in our future."

"Oh?" I kissed the top of her head. "What sort of game?"

"We do this, neither of us freaks out, keep your sexy math to yourself, and you show me what you meant when you bought the baby oil." She held out her hand. "Deal?"

Now that the wall between us had crumbled, all I could think was, *How did I miss this?*

How did I miss how cute she was?

How serious she was in this moment with just a bra and leggings on, her bare feet dangling near the floor as I carried her to the bed.

"Deal." I grabbed her hand and squeezed. "But you have to answer my question too...how do I look at you?"

"Well." Her eyes darted toward my mouth. "You

used to almost sneer when I'd walk into the room. Remember, we did almost kill each other planning Monica and Banks's surprise party."

The memory was painful.

Because it felt like that was what had triggered their deaths.

I hung my head. "I was jealous."

"Jealous?"

"You've always been this free, beautiful thing, and I was always jealous that I couldn't let myself be like that. I was irritated that you didn't seem to care about responsibility, and yet Monica and Brooks trusted you with raising their children. And I was always the too-serious one, the one that tried to keep everything one way, only to have you bulldoze your way into a situation and have a better, more exciting idea. Sometimes I blamed you for taking my family from me. You know how close Monica and I were, and then you just...became a part of our family, seamlessly, easily. Everyone loves you, you know. So I made myself focus on things I knew would put walls between us, and you know what you did?"

A tear slid down her cheek. "What?"

I swiped it away with my thumb. "You forced your friendship on me like a homeless cat that decides it's found its forever home."

She gasped. "You compared me to a homeless cat? You sure you're going to get laid tonight?"

"Yeah, I could have done better than that. It's just— you're just—how am I looking at you right now?" I asked for the third time.

Two more tears slid down her cheeks as she reached for my face and cupped my cheeks with her hands. "Like I'm yours."

"For two seconds I could have sworn you were going to say 'lobster.'"

"That too." She sniffled. "Even when I wasn't yours— I was yours, Rip."

I have no clue what the hell she was going to say next because I was kissing her, parting her lips with my tongue, while she grabbed my shirt and tugged it open, sending buttons flying all over the room.

I moaned inside her mouth when her hands moved to the buttons of my pants, I kicked them down and pressed her back against the mattress, leaning over her, almost petrified to stop kissing her, fearful of missing her even though she was right there.

Needing more even though it was physically impossible. Energy pulsed between us, around us, igniting each touch of our mouths to something almost holy.

245

She pulled back, mouth swollen. "What do you see when I look at you?"

I reached for the waistband of her leggings and slowly rolled them down her thighs, tugging them completely off as I answered. "Love. Acceptance...with a side of annoyance that I'm pretty sure I'll always see."

She threw her head back and laughed, then grabbed my face and pulled me down for another kiss as I unclasped her bra, freeing those perfect breasts. Releasing her lips, I drew back, holding her gaze with mine until I had to look away. I dropped my eyes to her chest and stared in wonder. I reached out. A blast of heat surged through my body as I weighed her breasts with my hands; they spilled over my palms, and a shudder of desire engulfed my body. She shivered as her tongue darted out to wet her lower lip. Body throbbing, I laved the soft skin around her nipples, then sucked one into my mouth and released it with a pop, watching as her chest rose and fell in perfect chaotic cadence with my own breathing, my own heartbeat.

As I moved to pin her arms above her head, she evaded my grasp and dropped her hands. She brushed the pad of her thumb over my tip, and I nearly died.

I quickly reached for the nightstand and grabbed

a condom. Her small hands continued exploring my length.

I growled, "Any more, and this is going to be over with before we start."

She gave a long-suffering sigh and licked her lips. "Next time, then."

"God, are you trying to kill me?"

"Yes."

"Why am I not surprised?" I laughed, moving her hands away so I could roll the condom down.

I grasped her knees and pushed them apart, crawling up her body. Her eyes fluttered closed in ecstasy as I nudged her entrance.

"Please don't be a tease in bed, please don't be a tease in bed," she muttered to herself.

"A little patience is good for you, Colby." Where was my renowned self-control now? It had abandoned me, and I was being driven by something feral, some primal instinct that beat, *Take her* in time with my heart's rhythm.

Everything about this moment felt like it had been ordained, and I had no idea why it felt so right, just that it did.

That *she* did.

"Rip!" She gritted her teeth, hooking her ankles behind me. My body loomed over hers, and I surrendered everything as I thrust into her. She threw back her head, lips parted.

It was the most beautiful thing I'd ever seen in my life.

Colby completely surrendering to me.

Trusting me.

I kissed the side of her throat, tasting her skin as she matched my rhythm, her body moving like it was made for me.

My muscles flexed taut as I tried to hold on, but every time I tried to rein myself in, she drew her nails down my back, or made a little mewling noise that was so fucking adorable I couldn't focus.

"Should have"—she groaned—"done this weeks ago."

"Months," I agreed. "Years."

"Yes!"

I molded her to me, willing the sensation of filling her to last, but I could tell I was already close, and she was almost there as I pumped one last time and felt her release around me.

My mouth covered hers in a soft kiss, and she cupped my face as the aftershocks of what we'd just done thrummed between us. I didn't want to pull out of her. I wanted to stay connected.

The most connected I'd ever been with another person in my entire life, and it was someone who used to call me Satan.

Someone I used to call immature and lazy.

Now all I could think about was that I had almost missed this.

"I know," she whispered.

"Did I say that out loud?"

"Yeah." Colby's bright eyes met mine. "I'm glad we didn't miss this too, Rip."

Our hands clasped and Colby squeezed tight. "What do you see now?"

I stared at our united hands and whispered, "The best damn trap I've ever been in, where my sneaky sister knew what she was doing, along with my best friend. A trap that's not really a trap but a dream. One I've wanted to be stuck in my entire life."

"Godparent traps are forever, you know...legally binding and all that," she teased.

"Good." I kissed her again, and again, then repeated, "Good."

TWENTY

Colby

I'd just had sex with Rip.

Sex.

And the first thought that came to my head was damn it, I wished Monica was still alive because she would be the first person I'd call.

And she'd always known I had a major crush on her brother. She'd made fun of me but always encouraged me, like she knew that we were perfect for each other. I swiped a tear from my cheek as I remembered our last serious conversation about Rip.

"He needs someone like you. Just don't give up," she said, *sipping her wine in the living room while the kids ran around screaming as Brooks played hide-and-seek with them.*

I frowned. "He needs perfection."

"Nah." She patted my hand. "Girl, he needs a big giant

mess that shows him how messy love can really be. He needs sinks to fix. Snotty noses to wipe. He needs the simplest moments in life that would normally pass him by if he stayed inside the box he's made for himself. He needs you."

Tears welled in my eyes as I looked away. "He won't ever see me as his perfect mess."

"Who ever said perfect was part of it?" She clinked her glass against mine.

"Besides, he thinks perfect *means control when it means the opposite. I'm pretty confident you can remind him of that, and one day he won't be able to help himself."*

I rolled my eyes. "Sure, OK."

A knock sounded at the door, and then Rip was walking in, holding a bottle of wine and saying hi to Brooks.

Rip's eyes roamed the room and landed on me. His jaw clenched.

"Remember this if you remember nothing else...," Monica whispered. "That's not anger I see on my brother's face."

"Oh yeah, then what is it?" I swallowed.

"Desire," she finished. "Now drink the rest of your wine, we have hide-and-seek to conquer."

And right now that major crush was naked in the bathroom, disposing of the condom. My heart and brain were not prepared for this! Breathe, just breathe.

I pulled the sheet up to my chest and peered into the door.

"I can see your reflection, Colby, it's creepy when you stare without saying anything."

I scowled.

"Saw that too."

"Nothing wrong with staring at a naked guy you just slept with when he has an actual real-life six-pack," I pointed out wisely.

The bathroom light flicked off. "How about establishing some rules?"

"Boo, I knew it, you're reverting back." Disappointment had tears forming in my eyes, and then I looked up just in time to see him pounce on me and jerk down the sheet until I was naked to the waist.

"Better." He nodded like he was proud of himself. "I have a lot to make up for, so I think that it's only fair the rule is, if I'm naked you're naked. Hey, if you get to stare, I get to stare, that's the rule. I'm naked, you're naked, I missed out on this for years...never again."

I pretended to think about it, but I wasn't an idiot. He was offering me himself. "I accept."

"Shall we shake on it?"

I held out my hand. He took it, then leaned down and pressed a gentle kiss across my lips that had me wondering how many hours we had before the kids were up.

"You look like you're scheming." Rip smiled.

My face heated. "Just thinking about putting NyQuil in the kids' juice boxes. You know, real parent-of-the-year-type stuff."

He burst out laughing. I'd forgotten how much I loved his laugh. Not that I'd heard it much over the years. But now that I thought about it...I'd been hearing it often the last week and more. I wanted to keep this moment forever, both of us free, laughing, talking about juice boxes, NyQuil, maybe even plotting a way to make a mean casserole. How was this my life now? And why was I suddenly so at peace? So happy?

"I love your laugh." I found myself sobering, reaching for his face. He was all flawless straight teeth, dimples, and a perfect jawline. So annoying.

But all mine.

"I love that you love it, Colby."

"For a frog you really can be romantic."

"Frog prince, get it right."

"Sure, OK..." I started moving away, only to have him catch me by the hips and pull me back. "That tickles!"

"Shhhhh." He kept tickling my sides. "If you wake up the kids you get to tell them about the cuddling."

I laughed harder. "Oh my gosh, you cuddled me so hard, do it again, Rip...pleeeeease."

His eyes dilated. "Whatever my princess wants."

"See, that's why the frog got kissed." I laughed as he ducked under the covers. "He said whatever she wants, whatever the princess wants..."

And he gave it. He gave himself.

TWENTY-ONE

Colby

We decided to get dressed in sweats even though it was three a.m., only because the last trauma the kids needed was to catch us "cuddling" in Rip's bed.

I was supposed to go back to my room hours ago.

But then I wanted wine.

Then he wanted cheese.

Then I needed a sandwich.

Then we grabbed some of the kids' Pedialyte—for obvious reasons—and then we started talking.

Or maybe we just started healing.

Rip pulled me against his chest. "Favorite classic movie?"

"*Casablanca*. Fight me."

"No fighting necessary, one hundred percent agree. Did you know that Humphrey Bogart was actually shorter than Ingrid Bergman? They had to put lifts in his shoes so he looked taller."

"Oh my gosh, you're one of those!" I slapped him on the stomach.

He frowned. "What do you mean, 'one of those'?"

"You're random-movie-fact guy!" I did a little dance next to him. "This means we're going to win every trivia game ever on any game night we participate in! Monica was always the worst at movie trivia!"

"She couldn't even quote *Friends*!" we said in unison.

"Brooks and I tried so hard with her too." He sighed. "At the end of the day you just hope you raise your children right, and, well, in the end you've gotta cut the apron strings and let them go."

I knew he was being semisarcastic, but Rip had basically raised her all on his own after their parents died when they were young. It wasn't something either of them really talked about. He'd been in high school, she'd been in eighth grade. Their parents had left them money and a house, and they'd had a distant aunt who'd lived with them, then moved out the minute Rip turned eighteen and took full parental responsibility. All they had was each other.

And me.

They'd always had me.

And then Brooks.

Banks.

Our friends had become our family.

"I'm glad it's you here with me," I whispered in a small voice.

His green eyes filled with moisture. "I'm glad it's you too, Colby."

"You weren't on day one of the great coparenting pact."

"I was grieving—I still am, and it just...was so much. I mean, it still is, but..." He gripped my hand in his, then lifted it to his lips. "Every day gets better."

"Every day does." I leaned in to kiss him and was interrupted by the pitter-patter sound of feet and whispering.

"I don't know, Aunt Colby wasn't in there. I looked!" Ben said in a panicked voice. "Aunt Colby!" His whisper was more like a yell, like he was scared something had happened to me. It broke my heart as I nearly tripped over the blankets to get to the door and grab Ben. No matter what happened, I'd never leave this kid—never leave them.

They were mine.

Just as much as they were Rip's.

And we were going to be the constant that they needed.

One Rip and Monica had never had growing up so fast after their parents died.

I cracked open the door to Rip's room and said, "I got scared, so Uncle Rip said I could sleep in his room."

"Cool!" Ben shoved his way in. "I wanna sleep in Uncle Rip's room."

He sped past me. Thank God Rip was fast, and he intercepted little Ben before he could jump onto the bed of fornication.

"Let's find your sister and we can go into the big bed together, sound good?" He winked at me, then sauntered sexily by.

I fanned my face and followed after him. Viera was still in the hallway, Bugsy tucked under her arm. She seemed to be staring into the shadows.

"What are you looking at, honey?" I asked, kneeling down next to her.

"Mom and Dad." She sighed. "They're angels now."

"Oh, are they?"

"Yeah, Dad said so."

I tried to keep my expression impassive when really I wanted to burst into tears. Was she really praying to her mom? Talking to her like I encouraged them to? It was almost too much to see the emotion on Viera's face and the pure confidence that what she said was reality. "Then it must be true."

"Ben don't believe me." Her lower lip trembled.

Ben let out a dramatic sigh. "I didn't say that!"

"Why don't we all try getting back to sleep and we can talk about it in the morning?" Rip intervened, and I released a relieved sigh.

Viera yawned while Ben just nodded as we all stumbled to the master bedroom and crawled into bed.

Rip flicked the lights off.

Within minutes the air was full of the kids' heavy breathing, but I was wide awake still—staring up at the ceiling.

Missing them. Monica and Brooks.

Wishing I could thank them for knowing me and Rip better than we knew ourselves and hoping to God they were looking down and giving each other a high five for being so wise and bossy.

Rip grabbed my hand and held it against his chest as we moved to cuddle, but the real kind, not the sex kind—we're not monsters.

"New normal," he whispered.

"New normal," I agreed.

TWENTY-TWO

Rip

"You look too happy," Banks pointed out the next day at work when I tried to avoid Heather like the plague. "Can I have the pears?"

I slapped his hand away, but that didn't deter him. He was right back there grabbing a damn pear like it belonged to him. He pulled out a chair and bit in.

Earlier that morning, Heather had given her two-week notice and left a fruit basket as a parting gift. I'd expected her to be somewhat upset over our conversation where I'd set clear boundaries, but I really hadn't expected her to quit over it—quite honestly I was thankful that the person who looked down on having kids and a family was out of my life. It just made me realize that maybe Colby was right, maybe people didn't change.

Then again, I'd like to think I had.

Banks picked up the card and snorted. "'I

appreciate you'? Is she serious right now? What sort of passive-aggressive bullshit is this? And why do you look so happy again? You never said..." He bit into the pear again, the noise like nails on a chalkboard.

"I'm always this happy," I said defensively.

Banks's green eyes narrowed. "No, you're not. You hate my mugs. You hate my ties. You hate color." I opened my mouth to argue, but he interjected, "One day you yelled at me for breathing too loud."

"In my defense you were hovering over my shoulder trying to read the *Men's Health* I was reading, and you were chewing in my ear!"

"Nice try. You're always grumpy, which brings us full circle to the weird smile on your face when I came in. I just had to say your name six times before the cloud of happiness dissipated around you. Normally you've got a billion different things going on, and right now, your laptop isn't even open."

My eyes narrowed. "Are you saying you want me to be a grumpy workaholic?"

It was his turn to narrow his eyes as he leaned in. "You kissed her, didn't you?"

I adjusted my bland black tie and wondered if I could shove his flamingo one into his mouth so he'd stop asking questions.

His smile grew and grew, until I was eyeing the pears and wondering how much force I'd need to knock him out with one. See, math, very handy, very sexy.

At least that was what she said last night.

"You're doing it again," he whispered. "And frankly, it's starting to freak Karen out."

"We don't have a Karen working here." I frowned.

"No, that's not her actual—" He sighed. "It's a figure of speech, I was teasing. And a Karen is like someone who gets upset over everything. You know, like they ask for the manager when their coffee gets too..." His voice trailed off.

"Damn it, who let you in here again?" I wondered out loud.

"And that is how friendship works, helping you see yourself more clearly even if it's so painful you want to strangle me." He held out his hand. "Friendship high five? No? Yes?"

I glared.

He changed the subject. "So is this why you have little hearts floating around your head singing Ginuwine?"

I frowned. "You and I have very different ideas of romantic songs. Doesn't he sing that 'Pony' song in *Magic Mike*?"

Banks just grinned. "Can't get any better than the 'Pony' song."

"I worry for your dating life sometimes."

"Don't. I do quite well. Besides, might I remind you that I'm the reason you're in this position. And you still haven't confirmed or denied coitus."

"Out." I pointed to the door. "You're giving me a headache."

Banks reached for another pear.

"Just take the damn basket!" I shoved it at him.

"It's my favorite fruit." He winked. "Oh, and Rip, I'm proud of you for letting your heart lead you to where your dick—"

"OUT!"

He just laughed and shut the door, and then he yelled through the crack. "You love me, man, one day you'll admit it!"

"Go annoy Heather."

He opened the door slightly and poked his head in. "Good idea, she might have more pears..." He shut the door again.

And for the first time in years, I sat at my desk and I worked with a smile the entire time.

Despite the maniac best friend who was stealing

pears and making me admit my feelings or lack thereof over the last few years.

I sent a quick text to Colby.

Me:

> Banks is in a mood today.

Colby:

> When is he not? Also, can you pick up some milk on the way home?

I don't know how long I stared at the text, smiling at the screen, touching it, then stupidly going through photos of the last few days with me, Colby, and the kids, and then going further back.

Photos of Monica and Brooks that I'd put in a special folder.

Ones that included Colby always smiling and laughing with Monica.

Ones where a lot of times I was staring at Colby or standing at the side in confusion, almost wondering why they were laughing so hard or loud.

The random picture would pop up where I was cracking a smile, but I always seemed tense, like I was waiting for the other shoe to drop.

And for the first time in my life, I didn't feel that way.

I felt free.

THE GODPARENT TRAP

I wanted to get the damn milk.

Bring it to Colby and claim a kiss before helping with dinner or putting the kids to bed right after, then catching up on all the moments she'd given me the opportunity to have.

That, like an idiot, I'd fucking missed.

TWENTY-THREE

Colby

"Aunt Colby, you did your hair!" Ben announced after jujitsu when I was running around the kitchen in a vain attempt to cook my very first pot of chili while Viera colored.

I'd wanted to surprise Rip with something that was gluten-free and actually tasted good.

And you'd think I'd wrestled Godzilla given how much I'd ended up sweating trying to get the house and kitchen cleaned up while at the same time making sure Viera didn't eat the glitter glue she was using in her latest masterpiece or more of the cat's food. Long story short, she'd been curious about the cat food, put some in her mouth, and then cried because she couldn't get it out.

She and Stu weren't exactly on friendly terms.

Stu chose that moment to walk by Viera's chair and meow.

Viera hissed.

Stu ran.

The world was backward.

Then again, so was our house, so, really, it made sense.

"Viera, don't hiss at Stu, it makes him sad," I sing-songed as I dropped the last can of chilis into the giant pot and stirred. "Hmm, not bad."

"That smells yummy!" Viera announced, choosing to ignore the hissing comment.

"Thank you!" I did a little dance in place while I continued stirring. Sure, the house didn't look sparkling, but the dishes were put away and the living room was in some semblance of order. I was learning that the best time for me to get things done was during and after afternoon nap. Once Viera was awake and had a snack, she liked to watch *Bluey*, which left me time to put the house back together. Today I'd even given myself some extra time to change before dinner. I'd put on different leggings, washed my face, put on some lip gloss, and combed my hair.

Things were looking up!

All moms should be sainted, I mean really.

Suddenly tears sprang to my eyes. I was living Monica's life, and while I was making it work, part of me felt—guilty.

I was cooking dinner in the kitchen she should have been cooking dinner in. I was waiting for the guy I'd always loved to walk through that door with a smile or possible scowl on his face.

I was getting ready in her bathroom because it had the best lighting.

I was kissing her children and tucking them into bed.

A tear slid down before I could wipe it away.

"I'm trying, Monica...I am..." More tears joined the first as I whispered into the stupid chili. "I'm so sorry."

I suddenly felt tiny arms wrap around my waist from behind. I turned around and looked down as Viera looked up at me, her curly hair shoved out of her face with a red headband that she'd refused to take off for ten days and counting. "I love you, Aunt Colby."

I sniffled. "I love you too, squirt."

"I no squirt! I big!"

"So big," I agreed. "You're right." I bopped her nose. "Can you show me your pretty picture?"

"Yay!" She sprinted back toward the counter and after two minutes finally managed to climb Everest aka her chair and sit comfortably. "Look! It's you, Aunt Colby." My eyes were x's, and I wondered if that meant I was actually dead. "And Uncle Rip." He looked worse, with teeth that were pointed and painted red. But we were holding hands—I mean, if you can call two lines crossing holding hands. "And Ben." He looked halfway normal, though he was missing an eye. "And Stu!" The cat was on its back with its legs in the air. No guess there; she'd killed the cat. "And Mommy and Daddy!" She pointed to two suns in the sky with eyes and what looked like wings. "My family," she announced proudly. "It pretty?"

My emotions were all over the place as I took the drawing from her chubby little hands. "It's the prettiest picture I've ever seen. We should put it on the fridge next to the others!"

"Yes!" She took ten more years to climb down from her chair, and then we were in front of the fridge arranging the alphabet magnets to hold the picture. It was perfect.

It was my family.

The door suddenly jerked open, and in walked Rip.

My heart nearly stopped as I rose to my feet and watched him walk toward me in slow motion. OK, maybe not slow motion, but it felt like it. He wasn't smiling, but he wasn't scowling either.

Did I hug him?

Did I shake his hand?

There was no manual for this, was there?

Just like there was no manual for losing your best friend and inheriting two perfect children while living with the one guy you'd loved forever but who was so out of reach you wondered if the sex was even real.

Because it was so unreal.

Rip stopped right in front of me while Viera made the long journey back up to her chair.

"You did your hair." He reached out, and I batted his hand away. "It looks nice." And then that gorgeous man flashed me such a perfect smile that my heart nearly stopped. "You look"—he leaned in and kissed my cheek, whispering, "beautiful."

My knees turned to jelly as I reached for his biceps and held on for dear life. I don't know how long we stood like that, me within inches of kissing him, holding on to him, begging him to lock the kids in the family room with a movie, then take me upstairs so I could kiss him, taste him, tell him about our day, ask him about his.

Get naked.

Viera sighed and threw her head back, smacking her hand against her face. "You guys are cuddling again!"

"Nah, we cuddled a lot last night, though," Rip said under his breath. I swatted him across the stomach.

He caught my hand and then kissed my wrist. "Viera, I have a surprise for Aunt Colby. I'll be right back..."

I quickly turned off the burner as he dragged me toward the downstairs bathroom and shut the door.

And then his hands were on mine, mine were on him, frantically pulling at his neck, bringing him close, tugging at clothes and wondering how fast we could do this with two kids under the age of six mere feet away.

"Missed you," he said between kisses. "So fucking much."

"Missed..." Our tongues fought for dominance. "Too."

"Need you." He tugged at my leggings, and within moments he had a condom on and me on the countertop. Rip surged into me with one big thrilling movement, filling me to the hilt.

He wasted no time in moving.

I wasted no time in holding on for dear life as he continued kissing me. Our mouths met, attacked. Pleasure flooded through my body with each violent thrust, and then I was there, gripping both him and the counter as I rode out wave after wave of my orgasm. He slammed into me one last time, my name the only word on his lips, and then he was resting his forehead against my shoulder.

"Hey, Rip." Why was I out of breath? I really needed to get back to the gym.

"Yeah?" He looked up at me, his green eyes lit with excitement.

"Best surprise I've ever been given." I laughed. "And now we have to hurry so the kids don't catch us."

"It's not like they know what we're doing," he said as he pulled out of me and grabbed a tissue to start cleaning up my thighs without me even asking.

I was still smiling when I pulled my leggings back up and realized last night we hadn't used a condom the second time.

"Rip!" Panic washed over me. "What if...what if the condom isn't enough? After last night, oh God, we can't handle more kids and—"

OK, yeah, I was high-key panicking for no reason because that was what I did when things were going so well, when they were so perfect, when I had this god of a man taking me against the bathroom sink.

"You're the only woman I've slept with in a year," he said softly. "And you're on birth control."

"How do you know that?" I stared at him in shock. Then I blinked. "And a year?"

"I was busy," he said, slowly eyeing me up and

down. "And I know because I know everything about you, even when I don't want to."

"I can't decide if that's romantic or mean."

He barked out a laugh and then said, "Let's go back into the kitchen and make sure Viera hasn't killed Stu."

"Oh, she already did."

He opened the door. "The hell?"

"Swear jar," Ben said in a bored voice as he walked by us with his iPad and headphones on.

"How did he even hear me?"

"She killed him in the picture she drew. I think I'm dead too. I can't tell, but x's over my eyes can't be a good sign, right?"

Rip grinned. "Yeah, probably not, since that's what the dead emoji looks like."

"Awesome." I took him over to the fridge. It was halfway covered with projects we'd been working on together as a distraction for the kids. They loved slime and they loved coloring. Ergo we had buckets of slime and scores of colorful crayons.

"What am I?" he whispered. "A vampire?"

"Uncle Rip, do yous love it?" Viera hopped off her chair and bounced over to us. "And can I know the secret?"

"Yes." Rip picked her up and kissed her on the head. "You're a great colorer."

She laughed and wrapped her little arms around his neck. "Duh, I know!"

"Humble too," I added.

"Yup." He looked over at me, his grin slowly falling from his face and something more intense passing over it.

He felt it too, didn't he?

The rightness of us in that moment, not just together in the kitchen, but together with the kids.

Well done, Monica. Even in her death she was still trying to matchmake me with her brother. And it was working. It was perfect. It was everything I'd ever wanted, I just hoped he felt the same way.

"I'm starving!" Ben moped into the kitchen and pulled out a chair. "Are we ordering pizza?"

"Nope." I went over to the chili and turned the burner back on to warm it. "I cooked!"

The kitchen went silent.

Rip set Viera down and then felt my forehead, earning a glare from me and a giggle from both kids.

I stuck out my tongue at Rip, only to have his eyes flash as he leaned in and whispered, "So inappropriate in front of the children, tsk-tsk."

I quickly grabbed a kitchen towel and started wrapping it in the air to create a whip.

"Run." I whipped it through the air.

He gulped and slowly started backing away and managed to find a towel of his own. "You sure you wanna do this?"

"Fight, fight, fight!" Ben started chanting. Viera joined in. Stu just sighed and probably pondered pooping outside his litter box. Yay me.

Rip moved to one end of the counter while I ran to the other end, ready to attack. We went in circles as the kids yelled, and then I bolted toward him, snapping the towel.

"Damn it!" he yelled.

"Swear jar!" the kids said in unison, and then Ben added, "I'm gonna be able to get my Bugatti soon!"

"How the h...eck do you know what a Bugatti is?" Rip asked.

"YouTube." Ben shrugged. "And some kid on Roblox has one."

Kids these days.

I laughed at the exchange and then realized that Rip had zeroed in on me. I held up my hands. "Now, Rip, be mature...remember what that's like? Where you don't have fun and iron your jeans."

He snapped the towel at me. "Weren't you the one that said you were bringing"—another snap toward my thigh—"me out of my shell?"

"Maybe tonight you go back inside it." I laughed.

He snapped the towel while I shrieked and jumped out of the way, and then he was grabbing me from behind while I screamed and the kids laughed.

"Cuddle her!" Viera shouted.

"Yeah!" Ben pumped his fist. "Say a bad word!"

I started laughing so hard I had tears running down my cheeks, the good kind, the happy kind, and as I wriggled around to face him, I could tell from the look on his face he was feeling the same way.

His smile was different.

Some might even say downright dazzling as he tilted my chin up and then pressed a deep kiss against my lips.

"Ewwwwwwwww." Ben groaned. "You're gross like Mom and Dad!"

"You hear that?" I said. "We're gross."

"So gross," Rip repeated. "Does this mean he's not dating until he's forty? Because I'm OK with that plan."

"I was thinking fifty."

"Deal." We both turned toward the kids.

Viera was grinning up at us like we were her world,

and Ben was counting the money in the swear jar, or attempting to.

Our kiss hadn't freaked them out.

If anything, it was the one normal thing they'd seen in the weeks since their parents' deaths.

And again it felt right.

Like things clicked into place.

I laid my head on Rip's shoulder and sighed. He wrapped an arm around me, and when he relaxed against me, I grabbed my towel and let it fly right against his thigh. "Gotcha."

Instead of attacking, he simply held me tighter and said, "Yes. You do."

TWENTY-FOUR

Rip

"She gave you a fruit basket?" She spit out the tooth-paste and then wiped her mouth with a towel. "Like with real fruit?"

How had I not noticed how gorgeous she was? How easy it was to exist around her? How attracted I'd been this whole time? And all the fucking energy I'd spent trying to push her away, to push away my feel-ings because they scared me, she scared me. Monica left. Brooks left. Our parents left. It was terrifying to suddenly allow yourself to fall so hard and fast that the idea of not existing with that person standing next to you, brushing their teeth, ruined you.

When I truly looked back and thought about it, I realized I'd just been irritated that they saw through me, every part. Monica and Brooks knew me better than I knew myself and knew what I needed.

I shook my head, bringing myself back to the present. "No, fake fruit, broke a tooth, lesson learned."

She rolled her pretty blue eyes and then pulled her dirty-blond hair into a messy bun and faced me. "I don't like her."

"I'm aware."

She put her hands on her hips, drawing attention to her smooth thighs and small black shorts. "Seriously, she's the devil, she was so freaking mean to me in high school, and I know I need to bury the hatchet, but she's...I'm sorry. This is me trying."

"Uh-huh." I was seriously distracted by the fact that Colby was wearing a black tank top with no bra. "I know you are."

She grabbed her moisturizer and started rubbing it all over her face and neck while I moved behind her to grab my toothbrush. That was when I realized... we moved together like we'd been sharing a space, a home, for years. Like we were always meant to be this in sync.

I moved out of the way for her when she reached across the counter, then handed her what she needed.

She snatched the toothpaste out of my hand as if we'd been doing this forever and put it away. "I just...I don't trust her."

"Are we still talking about Heather and the pear basket I gave to Banks?"

"Wait, why did you give it to Banks?" she asked, frowning.

"Banks has a thing for pears, and he was going to steal it anyway." I sighed and then started brushing my teeth while Colby hung up her towel and leaned her hip against the countertop.

"He needs to find the right girl and settle down before he turns into a contestant on *The Bachelor*, not that I'm judging, I'd watch the hell out of that."

I almost laughed because she sounded just like Monica in that moment. My sister had said the same to me more than once.

I pointed my toothbrush at Colby. "If you try to set him up with someone, he's just going to ask her cup size."

Colby gasped. "That bastard!"

"He's a player, told you so..."

"But he was always so nice to me," she argued. "Respectful."

I almost choked on my toothpaste as I spit it back into the sink. "Respectful? Colby, have you looked in a mirror recently? Any guy would think you were sexy as hell. Was he trying to play matchmaker? Yes, but don't for one second think that he wouldn't have jumped at the opportunity to get into your pants if he thought you were interested in him."

She sniffed and looked away. "You said I was a hot mess."

I pointed my toothbrush at her again. "Emphasis on hot."

Her cheeks pinked. "Anyway, he was just helping me out."

"Helping make me jealous, yeah, I know. Read that loud and clear every time he invited himself over and tried to take you out. Idiot. Did he really think I didn't notice you?"

She shrugged. "It seems to me that everyone around us knew this would happen and should, except for us. To be fair, our horrible date and sniping at each other for years didn't help."

I looked away, gripping the counter with my fingertips. "I was nervous."

She jerked her head up. "I'm sorry, what?"

"For our date." I licked my lips. "I'd been super nervous, and it was just easier to blame everything on your messiness than look at myself in the mirror and realize that maybe I was part of the problem, that my need to keep everything in little straight lines was an issue."

Her eyes softened. "Maybe we should just be thankful we figured it out sooner rather than later?"

"Mmm." I pulled her into my arms. "Agreed."

I kissed her forehead, the feeling so normal and natural that warmth spread through my chest.

We walked by the large bed. It felt wrong to get rid of it, but it felt weird sleeping with Colby in it knowing I'd probably be getting her naked where they...yeah, we weren't going there.

I followed Colby into my bedroom and turned off the lights once she got under the covers. "Sleep tight." I started to leave.

"Wait, where are you going?" She shot up out of bed.

I laughed. "Kidding, I just wanted to see your face."

A pillow came flying at me.

I caught it midair and then slowly joined her, pressing a heated kiss to her neck right below her ear. She let out a little moan and reached for me.

I sighed in contentment. "I really want sex right now, but..."

"You're exhausted," she finished for me, and then she yawned. "Me too."

"All the sex tomorrow," I promised, marveling at how we sounded like a legit married couple as I pulled her into my arms and then drew the covers over us.

Everything was falling into place.

Things felt perfect.

So why did I fall asleep with a feeling of dread and then have nightmares of something happening to the kids or Colby?

I was in a shit mood when I woke up the next day to see a calendar invite for a meeting this morning with Heather's dad. She'd set up the meeting, even after I'd told her I didn't need to discuss her father's job offer—even after she'd put in her two weeks. What was her angle? Something felt wrong, and I was afraid to say something to Colby; the last thing I needed was to freak her out after everything had been going so well. Besides, I only had a few more days of dealing with Heather.

I clenched my teeth and gulped down my coffee, ignoring my burned throat. It was supposed to be Colby's day to go in and get some work done, but that clearly wasn't happening, and I hoped she wouldn't get frustrated that she couldn't work until later tonight.

"Morning!" she said from the bottom of the stairs with Viera following close behind, Bugsy in one hand and Stu in hot pursuit, meowing.

Colby was wearing a large black sweatshirt and white leggings that looked amazing on her, her face was makeup-free, and her hair was pulled back into a low ponytail.

She looked really pretty, but then her smile fell when she saw my expression. "Oh no, did something happen?"

"No, not really," I sighed. "I need to go into work today. Heather made the appointment with her dad after all, and he's coming to my office. Unless I want to burn a bridge with one of the most powerful families in town..."

Colby deflated a bit. "You need to go. But no more fruit baskets!"

I slowly made my way over to her and set my cup on the counter, then took her hand in mine, linking our fingers. "No more fruit."

She scowled as I pulled her in for a hug, then kissed her forehead. "Trust me."

"You know I do." She smiled. "Just hurry home to us."

"I know how to handle her, all right? And tomorrow you can go to the office and work on your next blog post. I'm really looking forward to the Swedish meatball recipe."

Her head whipped up. "The only way you'd know that is if you follow my blog or Instagram."

I smiled. "Weird..."

"You followed me?" Her eyes filled with tears.

"Are you crying?"

She wrapped her arms around my neck so tight I started to choke. "You are so getting laid tonight," she whispered just as Ben came downstairs and demanded eggs.

"Well, that's a way to train me," I said back.

She stood up on her tiptoes and kissed my cheek. "Atta boy."

I grabbed her by the arm and pulled her back. "Oh, I'm sorry, did you think we were done here?"

She shrieked as I took her mouth, then noticed Ben roll his eyes again and mutter, "Gross" as he ran to the fridge and attempted to grab some eggs for her to fry. "Oh!" Eggs forgotten momentarily, Ben raised his hand like he was in class. "I got a hundred on my spelling test. Can I get ice cream this afternoon?"

"A hundred!" we both said at once. Even though he was great at spelling, he'd been struggling a bit with the double-vowel words, and we'd been practicing with him each night.

"Yup!" He ran for his Avengers backpack and pulled out a white sheet that had six spelling words on it and showed it to us. It had a "Good Job" sticker on it and the number one hundred written in bright-blue marker.

I held up my hand. "High five, buddy!"

He hit my hand, then Colby's.

"Tell you what." Colby bent down to his eye level. "Why don't I let Viera stay with Mrs. Harris for an hour, and I'll pick you up from school and we can go to Scream!"

His eyes grew as big as saucers. "But that's like super-giant ice cream cones ice cream!"

"And that's a big giant one hundred," Colby said. "So what do you think?"

"Yes, yes, yes, yes, I'm amazing!" He danced around us for a bit and then announced that he had to pee.

"Well, that was short lived," I said. "You sure you don't mind taking him?"

"Hey, I get ice cream too." Colby laughed. "I've got this, just go to work, change the world one tax deduction at a time."

"I really should wear a cape," I teased.

"Pretty sure the kids already think you have one, Uncle Rip," she said softly, bringing tears to my eyes, making it so I had to look away.

"Be safe, Rip." Her smile was full of joy, trust. I wanted nothing more than to come home to this every day. Damn it, I needed to figure out a way to take a sabbatical so we could finally heal, take the time and do it together.

As a family.

"You too," I choked out, and then I left, hating every step that took me further away from my future.

"I'm sorry," I said for what felt like the eleventh time. "I'm just not interested, Sam. I know you do amazing work, but I'm happy. I have a family that needs me, and if I started working for you and sold my firm, I'd be so busy I wouldn't get to see them."

Heather's smile was so fake I had to turn away so her father couldn't read the look on my face. The fact that she'd set this up behind my back pissed me the hell off. It put me in a rough spot with one of the most influential men in our city, one who wouldn't be beyond warning his friends away from giving me business in the future. And since Heather had never shared with him that she'd been the one to set up the meeting, not me, I looked like a flake for turning down his offer.

"I guess I just don't understand." He leaned back in the leather chair. "Heather said you were genuinely excited. What changed your mind?"

Heather gave me a blank look, because of course she did.

"Sir, with all due respect, I think we both had a mis-communication. I'm extremely thankful for the offer.

And would love to take it if I had more time, but right now I have things that are more important. I have a family to care for, kids who need attention, and while I'm sure Heather had the best of intentions setting up this meeting, I'm happy where I'm at. This isn't temporary." I paused to let Sam speak, but he was just looking at me in stony silence. "This lifestyle I have now, it's forever. My family needs me. And I need them." At that he nodded. "I am sorry that Heather is stepping away, she's been great." And she had been, but I wasn't sad to see her go.

Sam shot Heather a look that was less than pleased, and she looked down in her lap. "Son, I respect your decision, thanks for shooting straight, that's good business. If you ever change your mind, know I'll always have a spot for you, even if it means firing whatever idiot I need to hire next…"

Banks poked his head in. "Did someone say my name?"

Awesome. Perfect timing as usual.

To make matters worse, Banks was holding the mug that said, "I always swallow."

Instead of getting offended, Sam slapped his thigh and laughed. "Where'd you get that horrible mug?"

"This guy?" Banks asked. "I collect them."

Heather rolled her eyes as an idea popped into my head. "You know, Sam, Banks is one of the best accountants here, he'd be a great candidate if you're interested." Banks's smile turned panicked, as if he wasn't quite sure he could handle it when I knew he could. He was incredible. "Why don't you offer him the job?"

It would give me Banks in small doses.

And I knew that he liked money, and this job would triple what he was currently being paid since he wasn't a partner yet.

"In fact, as you know, Heather was already overqualified for her position. Why don't you hire them both? It's really the least I can do."

Sam nodded. "I like this idea. I need someone immediately. The last idiot missed a deduction and I had to pay an extra million on top of...well, on top of a lot of money."

"Sounds great." Banks's smile was genuine for once. "Why don't you come to my office tomorrow and we can chat? Better yet, I'll come to you."

"Great! And I like the idea of Heather coming back to the company. Gotta say I was really happy when she said she'd put in her two weeks, I always wanted to keep part of the company in the family. I only let her take the job here because she said you'd begged her for help." Sam nodded solemnly.

Well, that was interesting…since Heather had been the one to come to me and ask if I would hire her. Colby's words rang true in that moment.

Heather's smile was frozen.

I hadn't even needed a full-time receptionist, but she'd given me a sob story about how her father had fired her from the company.

She hadn't changed at all.

Just as conniving as ever.

"This has truly been a very eye-opening meeting." I said it to Sam but was looking at Heather. "I actually hadn't needed a receptionist, she said she'd been fired. I apologize for the miscommunication."

Her throat worked like she was having trouble keeping her perfectly polished smile in place. How had I ever thought I belonged with someone like her? What had I ever seen other than what she wanted me to?

Sam just shook his head. "I'm embarrassed, I don't know what to say, but I apologize. Heather, collect your things immediately, you're done today."

Heather said nothing and stomped out of the room. Her dad followed, and I felt actually sorry for him.

THE GODPARENT TRAP

Note to self, stop cussing so Ben can't get his Bugatti and become a spoiled kid like Heather.

Exhausted, I sat in my chair and checked my phone.

Colby:

How'd it go?

Colby:

She's showing cleavage, isn't she?

Colby:

I'll kill her.

Colby:

I mean really, should anyone be THAT pretty?

Colby:

I'm dying here. I have this nightmare on repeat of you taking her against the desk, throwing the stapler across the floor and just ripping her dress open and…

Colby:

Actually can we do that? I've always wanted to do that.

Colby:

...

Colby:

...I swear I'm not crazy.

Colby:

There's this song, I want to live in a world where all your exes are dead, and I feel it on a spiritual level.

I finally took pity on her and texted her back.

Me:

Let's not go to prison. It went well, more details when I get home, but know I miss you, and yes we can throw the stapler to the ground and have hot sex against my desk. Let's just make sure we do it after hours so Banks doesn't think it's an invitation to watch.

Colby:

Thank. God. And I want to say he wouldn't, but...the pear stealer would, he really would. Where did he come from, anyway?

Me:

No idea, he's like the friend that forces his friendship on you until you say yes and then wonder where it all went wrong.

Colby:

So he's me but male?

Me:

You didn't force yourself on me at all. And don't ever compare yourself to Banks.

Colby:

Ha ha kidding. Look at us adulting, we're so hot right now…I mean me, I'm finally adulting.

Me:

Burning up. And you already were adulting!

Colby:

It's getting hot in here. So take off all your clothes.

I burst out laughing. Leave it to Colby to make me laugh and change the subject. I quickly typed back.

Me:

You just aged yourself a bit.

Colby:

> How dare you, sir! I'm young and know how to use TikTok. Twenty bucks you don't even have it downloaded.

Me:

> I literally have seventy thousand followers.

It took her a while to text back.

Colby:

> I can't find you...

Me:

> It's too easy with you. Do I look like I dance in front of my own camera, then wait and see how many people think I'm legit?

Colby:

> Never say legit again.

I checked the time on my phone and sighed. I didn't want to stop talking to her. I could text her all day. But instead I had another meeting in a few with a new client.

Me:

> I don't want to go, but I have another meeting.

I typed "I love you" so many times that it was embarrassing, only to delete it because wasn't it too soon?

But I did.

I loved her.

And now I knew I always had. I had just been afraid to love someone I couldn't control. Someone who didn't fit in the perfect plan I had for my life, not even realizing that the perfect plan wasn't what I needed.

No, what I needed was someone who would push me, make me laugh, someone who wouldn't allow me to be a jackass just because my pencils weren't straight or things weren't going my way.

God, I'd lived such a carefully constructed life, and what had that gotten me? Misery. Math equations. And Banks, no offense to Banks.

Colby hadn't destroyed me.

She'd freed me.

I wanted to say it.

Say the three words. But over text? Was that lame? Why was I always overthinking things with the one person who probably wouldn't care if I said it via email?

I saw a few dots pop up and then get deleted on her end, only to have her finally just send a heart emoji, which nearly made mine stop.

I put my phone down and wiped my hands down my face. I had too many feelings and wanted to express them, but I wasn't free like her, I wasn't like her at all, so instead I just fixated on them.

What would Monica have said?

I laughed when I realized she'd probably smack me as per usual, then call me an idiot and walk off.

"Pretty accurate," I said to myself as I popped on my laptop really quickly and ordered Colby roses.

I might do things differently, but flowers always said *I'm thinking of you*, and she deserved to know that she occupied my thoughts, not just a few, but all of them, and I never wanted that to change again.

TWENTY-FIVE

Rip

I checked my watch again and then looked out the window. Colby still wasn't home with Ben. Things had been going so much better lately—hell, who was I kidding? Things had gone from a nightmare to perfection, making me wonder why I had been so hard on her to begin with. I'd let my own fears get the best of me, with her, with us, with everything.

Having a family was fucking terrifying, like giving up your heart every day and watching it walk out the door without protection. Add a girl you loved on top of two kids and I suddenly realized why so many parents were a hot mess. Warmth spread throughout my chest as I looked at Colby's shoes by the door.

Pink Nikes that used to drive me insane now made me smile and wonder why I was such a prick before. I mean, I knew why I had been a prick, it was to keep the one person whom I knew I wanted, who would challenge me and scare me. Out.

It was easier, wasn't it?

To walk through a carefully planned life where I didn't have to worry about serious relationships, love, things that could be taken away from me just like my parents had been, just like Brooks and Monica.

With a sigh I walked by the family picture of Monica, Brooks, and the kids.

It was the first time I was able to really look at the photo without getting angry, without feeling sorry for myself, without asking the universe why.

I could have sworn in that moment, as my sister smiled down at me, that she'd known. She had actually known that one day I'd be standing there staring at her photo and saying thank you.

Thank you for Colby.

Thank you for the kids.

Thank you for giving me the family I've always wanted but never dreamed I would have. And certainly never wanted to get this way.

I missed my sister and Brooks so much, but I wanted to believe they were watching over us. I wanted to believe what Colby told the kids. I wanted to believe that Monica and Brooks were looking down on us, wishing us well, thanking us.

I turned and eyed the picture that Viera had drawn, with her parents as angels.

I wanted to believe that there was more after death, that there was life, there was hope.

And that they watched us with annoyance as we stumbled around this darkness, this new life, and went, *Get it together, guys.*

"When you see a butterfly, think of me," Monica said with tears in her eyes on her wedding day, referencing our little agreement from when we were kids. "Butterflies mean that the world is shifting, by a simple flap of their wings they create ripples in the universe." She turned to me, her smile wide. "I'm not saying that anything will ever happen to me, but you need to know—I will always be by your side, ride or die, your little sister, forever. Regardless of my marriage or what happens in my future, know that I'm with you. It's us against the world. And if you ever doubt it, I'm manifesting this right now." She squeezed her eyes shut. "You'll know because you'll see a blue butterfly, all right?"

"Do I still get to be yellow?" I asked.

She laughed. "You remember."

"Always," I said. "How could I forget?"

She held out her pinkie to me. "So it's still a deal?"

"It's still a deal, baby sis."

I snorted because how ridiculous and whimsical could she still be? But also, I wanted in that moment to think that maybe there was hope, maybe our parents were looking down on us, maybe there was an afterlife where things were perfect. Where they weren't hard or sad.

As I took her pinkie in mine, I agreed, but I also doubted in my heart after so much loss in our lives.

Walking her down the aisle was one of the hardest things I'd ever done, and stupidly enough, just as we got to the minister—a butterfly flew overhead, as if to mock me or just prove her right.

I shook away the sad memory and walked by the kitchen window, then froze.

A blue butterfly was just outside the kitchen window, sitting on a flower, its wings flapping slowly.

My throat felt tight as I watched.

Within seconds it was gone.

Within seconds I had tears streaming down my face.

I quickly swiped them from my cheeks, embarrassed that something so small and insignificant could affect me. She'd been right this entire time, hadn't she? She'd always had so much faith where I looked at facts, and now, now I was the one standing there without her, staring at a butterfly.

"I hope you're well," I whispered in a gravelly voice as my phone started buzzing on the counter.

"This is Rip Edison."

"Hi, Mr. Edison, this is Mrs. Sue, I'm at the school with Ben, um, we've been waiting for over an hour, and Colby still hasn't picked him up. I tried calling several times, and it just goes to voice mail. Could you come grab him?"

Panic surged through me. Where was Colby? Was she OK? She was a lot of things, but she wasn't flighty enough to forget Ben. Never. "I need to grab Viera from her nap, then I'll be right there."

"Oh, I'm so sorry!" Mrs. Sue said. "Do you want me to drop him off? You already signed the paperwork stating I can do that since the funeral..." Her voice trailed off. "Since things have been difficult."

"Yeah," I croaked. "Actually that would be great, thank you."

"No problem! I just didn't want to do so without your permission. We'll swing by in a few minutes."

"Thanks." I checked my cell. No missed texts, nothing from Colby. My entire body went rigid. I wanted to default to anger because it was easier than the terror I felt that she wasn't where she'd said she'd be—and that she hadn't as much as texted.

She'd said earlier that she was going to work on her blog post, had she forgotten the time? It was something she'd do. I hoped to God that she'd just been in the zone, as she put it, because this was—this wasn't good.

"Unbelievable." I cursed under my breath and then remembered that Viera was upstairs sleeping. How the hell had Colby forgotten to pick up Ben, they'd had plans, and it had been her idea. The one thing she was supposed to do after grabbing groceries. In the deepest recess of my mind I knew I felt nothing but panic, but the anger was easier to focus on.

Please let it be something stupid.

I checked my phone again.

She was more than an hour late.

I tried calling her. No answer.

And then I called again, and again, and again, and then I finally left a voice mail. "Where the hell are you? Ben was at school waiting for you for an hour! His teacher has to drop him off, Viera's sleeping, and let me guess, you were saving a turtle as it crossed the road. Or decided to put your phone on silent and got distracted by something at the store. Please tell me that's the case, Colby. Please. What the hell? We've been doing so good, everything's been perfect. Fuck. Why aren't you answering? I'm trying not to freak out and I'm sorry I'm coming across as an ass, but I had this nightmare and please just call me back." I hung up the phone and then went to text messages.

At least then I could see if the message was delivered and read.

I quickly typed one out.

Me:

Call me please.

It said delivered but not read.

I tried again.

Me:

Look, I'm sorry for the voice mail. I'm out of my mind here. You know how Ben gets when nobody shows up. He freaks out and thinks something happened. You can't fucking do that to him so soon after his parents died. You can't do that to me, to us.

Again, delivered but not read.

I started to slowly panic as I recalled all the times I'd texted her or called. She'd always answered, she'd always responded.

With a curse I called Banks.

He answered on the first ring. "What up, dude—"

"Is Colby with you?"

"No." He drew out the word. "She stopped by to put a gift on your desk and then said she was going to the grocery store. I made a joke, she laughed, and then she left." Leave it to him to remember word for word what had actually happened. "Why?"

"She's not answering her phone, and she didn't pick up Ben. He's been waiting over an hour and obviously upset."

Banks was quiet, and then, "That's not like her."

"I know," I finally said. "Maybe she had car trouble?"

"She would have called." His voice sounded hollow. "Do you have the find-your-friend app on your phone?"

"Yeah."

"Is she on it?"

"No," I said, feeling dumb.

"Why the hell not?" he yelled. "She's not just your friend, Rip. For shit's sake, you know the only reason I showed interest was so you could pull your head out of your ass and see what was right in front of you the entire time, at the very least put her on your app so you can find her."

"I know." My voice cracked. "I know. And she's not

answering. And we just started..." I sighed. "And she's not fucking answering!"

"Calm down." Banks cursed. "Look, I'll make some calls. She's probably fine."

Probably.

That's what I had thought about Monica and Brooks.

That's what all of us had thought.

And I'd seen that damn butterfly, and now I was freaking the fuck out that something was wrong.

The doorbell rang. "Someone's at the door. I'll call you back. Or you call me if you hear from her."

I hung up the phone and ran to the door, jerking it open to a sobbing Ben and an apologetic Mrs. Sue.

Her bouncy blond hair made her look even more cheerful as she ushered him into the house and said, "He's worried."

That made two of us.

"Buddy, don't worry, OK?" I knelt down on the floor and pulled him in for a hug. "Aunt Colby probably forgot her phone somewhere, OK?"

I hated that I was lying.

I couldn't feel my legs, and I had to be strong for him, for both of the kids, when I couldn't even be strong for myself. It was my worst nightmare.

Was that why I'd seen the butterfly?

Fresh waves of panic washed over me until I felt like I was going to puke.

He sniffled. "O-OK. But she promised to pick me up and we were supposed to get ice cream, remember? And she promised, she promised this morning. Something's wrong." He continued to sob against my chest. "Did she die? Did she die like my mom and dad?"

I was going to kill her, then kiss her senseless once I found out where she was, because I would.

There was no way the universe would do this to us again. Right?

Right?

"I'll just go," Mrs. Sue mouthed, and she quickly left.

I nodded and pulled Ben close. "Hey, why don't you go grab a snack from the pantry while I try calling Aunt Colby again?"

Could he feel my panic? The way my body shook with fear?

He sniffled. "Can I have candy?"

I sighed. "Yes, but only two pieces, and nothing with red coloring in it. You know how it makes you go crazy."

He pouted. "I wanted the Swedish Fish."

"Well, you're gonna get the yellow gummy bears instead."

He made a face. "Nobody likes the yellow."

"Hey, I like the yellow ones!" I argued, earning a grossed-out stare from Ben as I looked down at my phone, willing it to ring. Willing my heart to stop racing.

I tried calling her again.

And again.

And then, when I'd started losing all hope—she answered.

"Colby?" I yelled. "Where are you?"

"S-sorry." Her voice seemed far away. "It's been a hard day."

"'A hard day,'" I repeated. Seriously? That was all she had to say? "Colby, Ben was worried." I had been worried, but I didn't say that. "I called, I texted. What the hell?"

She made a noise that sounded like she was in pain, and then the sound of something dropping hit my ear.

"Colby? Colby!" I yelled.

Nothing.

The line went dead.

What the hell was going on?

I didn't even have time to figure it out because Viera started bawling from her room. I ran up the stairs to grab her.

Viera's room was a mixture of pinks and purples,

with twinkle lights next to her big-girl bed. Another thing that Colby had added, because she thought the glow of the lights would make Viera feel safer.

"Hey, baby girl." I reached for her just as she raised both hands out to me, then lifted her from the crib as she clung to my neck. She started sobbing all over again. "Hey, hey, it's OK…"

"Where's Aunt Colby? I want Aunt Colby." *Me too*, my heart pounded, even though I was pissed at her, I wanted her too. My stomach sank to the ground.

"She'll be home soon," I lied. "Let's go get a snack, OK?"

I pulled her into my arms and carried her down the stairs. Ben was already eating his fruit snacks and playing Roblox on his iPad when we made it down to the kitchen.

I had set Viera in her high chair and was going to grab something to eat when my phone finally rang.

I snatched it up. "Hello?"

"Is this Rip Edison?" asked an unfamiliar female voice.

"Yes." My heart started to pound out of control.

"Oh good, I'm calling from Mercy Grace Hospital. There's been an accident. I'm calling for Colby Summers."

TWENTY-SIX

Colby

I'd finally made a plan and outlined my day. I was going to work for the first half of it and then run house errands, which I successfully did, yay me! Then I was going to go pick up Ben and take him out for a special afternoon. I was so freaking proud that he had worked so hard on his spelling test, and I knew Monica and Brooks were smiling down at him, at us.

I wanted to spoil him, tell him how amazing he was, how smart, how brave. I wanted to shower him with compliments, then have dinner with Rip—with my family.

I was grinning like an idiot as I drove toward Ben's school, until I saw that traffic had suddenly stopped.

Frowning, I put the van into park and looked out the window.

There was a van ahead that was on fire. One much

like ours, and people were screaming, a little girl was waving out the window, and people had stopped on the side of the road, all of them on their phones.

Is this how it happened to Monica and Brooks?

Did they scream?

Were they waiting for someone to save them?

Tears filled my eyes and spilled over as I opened my car door and started to run. I had no clue what I was doing or why, but I had to save them.

I couldn't save my best friends.

But I could save these people.

I could give them a second chance.

I could hear Monica's voice. "Help them."

I could see Brooks's smile. "Save them."

I ran so hard, so fast, that I don't even remember the time it took for me to hit the pavement next to the car and look inside, people screaming at me to back up, to move because there was no hope, the car would explode, they would die, and so would I.

Ignoring them, I was able to open the door and reach across as pops and cracks sounded all around me. Glass pierced my skin, but I continued reaching across the other seat.

A screaming toddler was still in her booster.

Through the smoke and tears I tugged at her seat belt and got her loose and thank God another Good Samaritan was already waiting outside the car.

An elderly Black man wearing a postal uniform was holding out his hands. "Give her to me!" he yelled.

I did. I handed her over and went for the mom.

She was completely passed out, so much blood on her face that I couldn't even decipher what she looked like.

The airbag hadn't gone off, so she'd hit the steering wheel hard.

Her manicured hands were still gripping it so tightly that I wondered if I was going to be able to even pry her away.

An explosion went off in the rear.

"Hurry!" the man yelled. "You have to hurry!"

"OK, OK." Why was nobody else helping?

I unbuckled the mom's seat belt and started to pull her out. She didn't wake up, but at least she wasn't stuck on anything.

"Colby!" the man yelled. How did he know my name? "You have to hurry. You have to be strong, OK? I need you to hurry."

"I'm trying." I coughed from the smoke. "She's heavy, I don't know if I can do it!"

"You can," he said in a much calmer voice. "You can do this."

"I can do this," I repeated, swallowing past the lump in my throat.

I tugged her harder.

Visions of Monica and Brooks filled my head.

Of them fighting for their lives.

Of sirens and the sound of metal crushing metal.

Something cut through my thigh as I kept pulling this woman out, this mother, this mother who was just like Monica, who deserved a second chance.

Another popping sound had me shrieking as I gave another tug and then another, we were almost halfway out when the loudest boom I'd ever heard sent us sailing away from the car and across the pavement.

In a daze I looked over and saw that the woman was free, but my body felt off, different, my arm wasn't in the right place, my legs felt like they were on fire.

I looked up into the sky, wondering if this was it.

If I'd finally found my forever.

Only to lose it forever.

"Rip." I whispered his name. I had to. I had to say his name, to know that if I was going to die right now, at least I'd die with his name on my lips.

I was falling in love with him.

I was terrified to tell him.

But I loved him.

This wasn't supposed to be our ending.

Hot tears slid down my cheeks as I started to sob.

And then, magically, my purse was next to me and my phone was in my hand, and the man who'd helped me before looked down and smiled. "You're going to be OK."

"I think I'm dying," I whispered. "I know I'm dying."

"No. You aren't. You'll be OK, Colby. Have a little faith…"

My vision was blurry, but the last thing I remember is his smile.

It was beautiful.

So beautiful I smiled back.

"Stay with us!" a new voice said. "Stay with us!"

Sirens sounded around me. "Wh-where am I?"

"Ambulance," a male voice said as I tried to shake my head clear. "You've been in an accident…"

"But what about the man? That postal worker?" I groaned. "Did he call you guys? What about the family?"

"Ma'am," a female voice said sternly. "There was no post office truck or man at the scene, only you and the mother and child you saved."

"No, no, that's not right. He was there."

"Ma'am...there was no truck and no man. You're injured, try to stay still."

I thrashed a bit more and squeezed my eyes shut, only to realize that the name on the man's uniform... had been Brooks.

TWENTY-SEVEN

Rip

Mrs. Harris had annoyed me in the beginning, because she seemed nosy, but really she cared, and I knew that. She always dropped off meals, always asked how we were doing, and took care of the kids when I needed her, and right now?

I needed her.

She didn't even ask questions, just told the kids they were going to make cookies and took them into the house like nothing was wrong, then touched my arm before I was able to walk away and said it was going to be OK.

I couldn't focus as I drove toward Mercy Grace.

The same hospital that I'd had to go to with Colby that awful day, the same hospital Colby was currently at, in critical condition.

A car accident.

Her running toward danger.

What the hell had she been thinking?

I was a numb mess as I parked in the ER lot and ran toward the double doors. Everything came back to me about that day.

Colby'd held my hand, hadn't she?

I stopped before the doors and remembered the last time I'd stood outside this hospital.

"Hey." Colby gripped my head with both hands. "We're going to make it through this, we're going to be OK because we have to be OK."

How had I never seen how amazing she was? How she had things way more together than I ever had?

I walked through the hospital doors and went to registration, body numb. "I'm here to see Colby Summers."

The elderly woman looked up and smiled. "Let me just see, oh yes, she just got out of surgery, she's in—"

"S-surgery?" I blurted. "She was in surgery?"

The woman offered me a sad smile. "I'm sure her doctor can update you on her condition. She's a very lucky girl. You're going to just walk down the hall, take a left when you have no other option, and on the right is the ICU. The nurses there can direct you, OK? I hope she feels better soon!"

"I hope she feels better soon"?

She was in the fucking ICU!

I was out of breath as I sprinted down the hallway. Two male nurses were standing at the ICU desk, each with a clipboard in hand.

"I'm here for Colby Summers," I blurted, eyes searching each of theirs.

"She's in room 1107," the younger one said. "But I should probably prepare you..."

"Prepare me?" I repeated as dread washed over me. I was too late. "Prepare me? For what?"

"She has a concussion," the other said. "We think it's related to the swelling around her brain, but you're going to need to be patient with her as she regains her memories for the next few hours, possibly days. It's hard to tell with brain injuries, but she seems to be in the clear, no internal bleeding."

"OK," I found myself saying, even though none of this was OK. Even though I was far from OK. I was going to lose my damn mind. How was this happening? I was just in bed with her this morning. I'd just kissed her. She'd slapped me on the ass, then tried chasing me around the room. I'd called her crazy and then we'd ended up kissing again. "Can I see her?"

The younger one moved around the counter and said, "Follow me."

I tried to keep my head down, to keep my eyes averted because everything reminded me of being here and identifying bodies and if I didn't compartmentalize I was going to lose my mind.

I was finally at her room, pushing the door open, when I saw her face.

It was covered in bandages, along with her head, part of her right arm, and both of her legs.

Tears filled my eyes as I moved to sit next to her.

She stirred a bit and then flashed me a doped-up smile. "Hey..." She frowned. "Where's Monica?" Her brow furrowed. "Wait, that's not right, is it?" Tears filled her eyes. "She's not here..." A tear slid down her cheek. "They're gone, aren't they?"

I wanted to scream, then cry all over again, because the beautiful girl in front of me with her worried smile and tear-filled eyes was about to get her world thrown a second time as I confirmed her worst fears.

TWENTY-EIGHT

Colby

I woke up to see my nightmare staring back at me.
Oh, who was I kidding? He was a walking dream, an
Adonis who was staring back at me like I was a complete stranger, which was silly, since he was my best
friend's brother.

And I was completely in love with him.

Had been for years, the only man I saw when I
thought about my forever. Too bad he hated me. I
mean, it wasn't like I meant to spill wine all over him
or annoy the crap out of him.

Something in the back of my mind told me that he
really did love me, that he always had. The way he held
my hand was so familiar, like we'd just been doing it a
day ago. I knew I should remember, but couldn't.

I knew Monica wasn't here and couldn't be.

I knew something was wrong, and this was Rip, my

Rip. He'd said so, when was that? A few days ago? Last year?

Tears of frustration ran down my cheeks.

"I feel like shit," I admitted, staring down at the fresh bandages on my arm and legs and trying to ignore my headache. "I'm confused but know I shouldn't be. Somehow you look worse than I do." I narrowed my eyes against the sting of tears that threatened to fall.

He swallowed slowly, his eyes glassy as he reached for my hand. "Are you in pain? Do you need a nurse?"

"No, they have me pretty high on morphine right now. Apparently I saved a little girl and her mom...I don't remember much about what I did, but the doctor that's on shift said it was going to be on the news, some sort of miracle, I guess." I started to feel even worse when he suddenly burst into sobs and laid his head down on my bed.

I don't know what possessed me, the old me would have never done this, but I yearned for him. For what we had, even though I was confused about how I was so certain. It's like my body knew. My soul agreed, and my heart couldn't help but love him even if nothing in that moment made sense. I reached out with my good hand and ran my fingers through his hair.

It was familiar and then it wasn't.

Had I touched his hair before in my dreams? Or was this something real? It felt real in that moment, just like his touch, his tears, just like the death of my friends, which I remembered with sudden clarity, as if it had just happened.

I kept doing it, because it was feeling more and more familiar, and then he moved, pulling me gently into his arms.

"You were right," he whispered. "I should have grieved."

"Grieved? Rip, I'm fine." I almost asked him if I should call Brooks or Monica, then remembered, they weren't here, were they?

"Just let me hold you for a while."

"You hate me."

"I love you," he fired back. "I've always loved you."

My heart slammed against my chest as goose bumps rose all over my body.

"It's never been hate," he whispered against my neck, causing chills to run down my spine. "It's fear. It's fear of letting go, losing control, it's fear that something's going to happen to you, so yes I scold you, yes I get angry, but the anger just masks the pain, Colby. It masks the guilt that my parents aren't alive, and it masks the guilt that—that—"

"How's our patient doing?" the doctor on shift, something Jennings, swept into the room and stood behind Rip. "I just need to check her really quick, sir."

Rip didn't budge.

"Sir?"

"I'm not letting her fucking go." He gritted his teeth and held on tighter like he was afraid of losing me.

"Sir, please don't make me get security, I need to check on my patient. I promise you can stay here the entire time."

"Rip, it's OK," I soothed him, trying to grapple with my own emotions coursing through me and the memories hitting me full force of our life, of almost losing what we'd finally found.

Finally he moved away and glared at the doctor. Ah, that was the Rip I remembered.

The doctor cleared his throat and said, "I'm assuming this is your partner? He's very protective."

"Oh no, no, we aren't—"

"Yes," Rip said. "I am."

My eyes widened. I would have 100 percent remembered that, head injury or not. "Rip, what are you—"

"We have two kids."

Tears spilled over my cheeks. It was true. All of it, except the whole asking to be my boyfriend or partner thing. We did have two kids. Two beautiful kids. Two gorgeous kids we couldn't even take credit for but would raise the hell out of.

More memories assaulted me until I started seeing spots.

"They're ours," he continued. "We're a family. Or we will be, once Colby gets better and can come home. She's literally the worst cook on the planet, despite her uncanny ability to blog about food and shovel it down about as fast as she can type. At least she has mean coloring skills." He took a breath and kept going as tears ran down my cheeks.

I cried harder.

I'd colored with Viera after they died. After Monica and Brooks left us.

After the fights with Rip.

After the making up.

The horrible chicken.

The lovemaking.

"The youngest likes to draw pictures of killing the cat. Don't worry, they just have a weird war going on, may the strongest survive and all that." He smiled at me while the doctor moved to check my IV.

At this point I couldn't stop staring at Rip. My forever.

Mine.

A year ago I would have asked if this was some cruel joke about the life we could have if he pulled his head out of his ass.

"I didn't realize I would be that protective of a dad until the oldest had a jujitsu match and I felt the need to go talk some sense into the little shit that was mean to him." He smiled at the doctor, who looked at him with polite awkwardness.

The memory of Rip running out onto the mats flashed into my head.

Rip running through the gym.

A kid having attitude.

Was it a dream?

It felt like a dream.

But I knew it was true.

After all, hadn't I been the one trying to film it on my phone?

I laughed despite the tears. "Still going to post that video."

"Thank God." Rip reached for me, doctor be damned. "I finally found you, Colby. Please," Rip pleaded. "Please remember us. Remember your forever." He pulled something out of his pocket and handed it to me.

It was a small picture of demons.

It said, "my family."

I smiled down at the cute page as a tear fell onto it.

"Mom and Dad are angels," Viera said at bedtime. It wasn't the first time she had said that. "They talk to me at night, and Mama says that she's safe."

"Great, honey, I'm so glad you're not as sad as before."

"Sad? Nope. They real! I knows it!"

"Even better." I kissed her head. "I bet your mom and dad are the best angels in heaven."

"Duh." She laughed.

My memory flashed forward to the sirens, and then dialing Rip of all people before my phone was taken away from me. I said a few words to him, he was yelling.

And then I heard voices.

So many hushed voices about my vitals.

My body gave a jerk as I slowly looked over at Rip, at the tears staining his cheeks along with the smile he saved only for me. Other than a few bandages and the horrible headache, I suddenly realized I'd escaped pretty unscathed, all things considering.

"Are the kids"—I burst into tears—"are they OK? I'm so sorry, I just, I couldn't not react, Rip! I remember, of course I remember, it was just a bit fuzzy."

"That's normal." The doctor started talking until

Rip shot him a glare that said to shut up and stop ruining our moment.

Rip moved around the doc and pulled me into his arms again. "You remember the kids? You remember—"

"How could I forget our crazy, chaotic life? The doctor said some memories might be fuzzy or feel strange as I heal over the next few days. I'm so sorry, I'm so sorry." I sobbed against him.

Dr. Jennings cleared his throat. "I'm going to give you some privacy. Your neuro checks are coming back to normal. It appears like the swelling's gone down significantly. We weren't sure if it would be a few hours or a few days." He started to walk away, and then called back, "Your family sounds perfect."

I thought back on the chaos and whispered, "It is."

Rip

One Year Later

Colby was going to drive me to drink.

And I loved her.

But I mean, sledding? At six months pregnant?

I tried not to lose my mind when Colby toppled over in two feet of snow.

She was fine.

It was all fine.

I was going to turn into a helicopter fiancé if I didn't rein it in. She waved over at me, I waved back.

"Losing your shit." Banks hit me on the back and handed me a cup of coffee. "Don't worry, I spiked it." He waved at Colby. "She's the best."

"Mine," I growled.

"I know, that's why I gave you this mug."

I looked down and groaned. "Will do chores for a BJ."

EPILOGUE

"Great." I sighed.

Banks motioned her over while Ben and Viera started building a snowman. When she approached, he grinned and then ran off toward the kids. He was incorrigible.

But it was nice to keep him around.

After the accident it had taken a while for Colby to recover physically, and we'd both shed tears over the random man with the name Brooks.

I'd thought her accident would set me back.

Instead it helped me grieve in a way I'd never been able to before.

Because now I knew that nothing was promised.

It was often messy.

But worth it.

I didn't have all the answers.

But what I did know?

Life isn't easy.

But it's good.

So damn good.

"Nice cup." Colby crossed her arms. "You trying to send me a message, Rip?"

I held it up. "Nahhh."

"Consider it received." She laughed. "Damn Banks and his mugs!"

"You love it."

"So do you." She elbowed me as the kids tackled Banks to the ground. "Well, we went from no kids to three."

"Yup." I took a sip and winced. "That's a splash of coffee and a whole lot of something else."

"Banks," we said together.

"He's your best man for a reason," she pointed out. "And I'm your best woman because you're going to get lucky again tonight."

"I better. I'm holding this stupid mug."

"Is that why you're smiling?"

"No." I smiled wider.

The kids shrieked, then waved as Mrs. Harris came out with her chair and a billion layers of clothes on to watch them. She'd been instrumental in helping us as Colby healed.

And another piece of the puzzle had come together.

The kids called her Grandma now.

And since she'd never had kids, well, it was like the perfect fit.

Joy can follow sorrow.

"Kids!" Heather walked out of our house with an apron on and yelled, "Time for dinner!"

Her dad sped by her, bent down, and sent a snowball

EPILOGUE

flying toward Banks's face while Heather touched her swollen belly.

"Truth." Colby sighed. "Stranger than fiction. It's still weird they're together, am I right?"

"She just needed someone like...him."

Banks started another snowball war while we all laughed.

Until a snowball came flying toward my face, compliments of Banks, and it was on. "Sorry, best friend!" Banks yelled. "It slipped."

"Slipped, my ass," I ground out. "Here, hold this." I handed Colby my mug and, for the first time since I was a kid, decided to beat a friend's ass in a snowball fight.

"Uncle Rip!" Viera screamed. "Look! I made a butterfly in the snow!"

I stopped my assault and looked over at Colby.

And smiled.

Acknowledgments

This may sound like I'm repeating the same thing over and over again, but man, I'm so thankful to God that I'm able to write and live my dream. SO. Thankful. This book truly would not have gotten finished without my husband and all his help. I was writing it during a pandemic on top of attempting to adopt again, and let's just be honest, having a six-year-old at the time, at home, bored out of his mind, didn't help things.

I'm so thankful to Amy Pierpont (my editor), who was so patient with me, and to Sam, whom I probably sent way too many emails to! You guys were the best, and I love working on projects like this with you where we can brainstorm!

Thank you to Trident, and Erica Silverman, for believing in this story and getting the ball rolling! To my assistant, Jill, ha ha, we also brainstormed a very long time over this, and it was so much fun, and such a fun way to take the chaos of the pandemic and kids at home and put it into a book where I could be like, oh no, that actually happened, that's not fiction, bro.

ACKNOWLEDGMENTS

I always lack when it comes to my acknowledgments because just like it takes a village to raise kids, it takes a village to get a book out there! Thank you to everyone at Grand Central. To my amazing beta readers and to Rachel's New Rockin' Readers, the best group on Facebook (I'm totally biased, I know), if you want to connect with other readers in a bully-free zone, we got you! Readers, bloggers, Valentine PR, and the amazing Nina Grinstead and her squad, you guys are amazing, thank you for all your hard work. And to the bloggers reading, the readers supporting, I'm always so freaking thankful that you take a chance on me!

Thank you so much!

HUGS,
RVD